HOWL

Micah Hales

Dedicated with love to August, Charlie, and Lucy,
(Meet you at the lake. Keep the towels in a sunny spot.)
and to Tore, Somerset, and Matilda,
with all of my heart.

This is a work of fiction. Names, characters, places
and incidents are either products of the author's imagination
or, if real, used fictitiously.

ISBN: 978-1-7330494-0-5

Printed in the United States of America

First Printing, June 2019

www.micahhales.com

Acknowledgements

Thank you to everyone who supported me through the writing process with insightful notes and feedback: Tore Knos, August Hales, Katherine Whiteside, Michele Zebich-Knos, Tore Knos Sr., Michael Hales, Christine Simoneau Hales, Aron Flasher, Mollie Lief, Isolde Motley, Gregory Colbert, Glen Hommy, Chloe Muller, Erica Murphy and Coco Barrett. Thanks also to Hannah Fasick for her excellent editorial work, Ronnie Datta for his cover illustration, Meghan Joseph for her creative eye, Bryan K. Reed for his beautiful formatting and cover design, and to Colin Francois for his enthusiastic support and endless promotional ideas. And last but not least, big kudos to the Crunchy Potatoes for all their support and general awesomeness.

Table of Contents

1. Camp Glynwood

Celia had begun planning her escape back to New York City before she'd even arrived at Camp Glynwood. It was a three-hour bus ride from Manhattan's Port Authority to the Catskill Mountains, and while the other girls giggled and chattered with excitement about the four weeks that lay ahead, Celia counted and recounted her money for a return ticket.

At the sun-drenched Greyhound bus station in Phoenicia, New York, Celia snagged a return bus schedule from an information kiosk. Then she crammed herself into the last available seat on a rickety camp van that would take her the final short stretch of the trip. She paid careful attention to the names of the dirt roads that led back to the bus station, and the distance according to the van's odometer. Left on Carpenter Road, right on Lark's Way, left on Glynwood Lake Road—except all in the reverse—5.4 miles total. No problem. She would leave tonight.

When the van, which was booming with the off-key wails of unfamiliar camp songs, *finally* reached Camp Glynwood, Celia let the girls, already-barefoot, barrel past her to pile out of the vehicle. Once the way was clear, she cautiously climbed out of the van and looked around. Camp Glynwood was for girls ages seven to fifteen, and by Celia's age of eleven, some of her fellow Glynwood Girls, as they called themselves, had already spent five or six summers together. Celia, however, didn't know a soul.

She'd anticipated feeling out of place in the upstate mountains with her skin the color of dark hot chocolate before you add the marshmallows, and her wild, giant puff of black hair barely tamed into braids—but as she scanned the scene before her, she was pleasantly surprised to see extra dark, medium, light, and beyond pale complexions, with every hue and texture of untamed hair, running toward each other, hugging and squealing in delight.

A woman plopped Celia's duffle bag down in front of her.

"Phew!" she huffed, pretending to wipe a sweaty brow. "You know we've already got a kitchen sink here, right?" she joked.

Celia looked the woman over. She was in her mid-twenties, with lightly tanned skin and perfectly white teeth drawn into a struggling smile. They were about the same height.

"And you are…" the woman ducked her head to read Celia's name tag, "…Ceee--li--a?"

"That's me," Celia answered, quickly stuffing the return bus schedule into her pocket to shake the woman's extended hand.

"Welcome to Camp Glynwood!" the woman practically sang. "I'm Susan, the Camp Director." Then she quickly checked something off on her clipboard which had materialized out of nowhere.

"Let's see, Celia Johnson…you're in Dorm Lucky Number 13. It's down the Hedgehog Path, just to the right of the Meeting Rock."

"Thanks, Susan," Celia said glancing in that direction. Her hands felt useless and huge. She hitched her thumbs into the smallest pockets of her jean shorts. But this made it look as though she was shrugging her shoulders, which was rude, so she immediately took them out again.

"There's a snack table set up by the Chow Lodge," Susan continued, "and a Meet'n'Greet for new campers over by Command Central. That's what we call the main office," Susan said winking.

"Thanks, Susan," Celia said again, this time just standing with her arms to her sides like an awkward robot child receiving orders. Susan tucked her clipboard under her arm and glanced at her wristwatch.

"Feel free to roam around and get the lay of the land," she said. "We'll gather at the Meeting Rock at 5:00 pm. You'll hear the Time Gong sound off five times." She motioned to a gigantic metal gong hanging between two trees. "That's how we keep track of time around here."

"Thanks, Susan," Celia said instantly regretting regurgitating the same two-word sentence three times in a row. She rested her gaze just above the treetops, but then she thought this might look like she was rolling her eyes, so she shot Susan a laser-beam stare and tried to smile.

Thankfully, out of nowhere, a pack of barefoot girls came hurtling toward Susan. It was hard to tell how many girls made up the wild tangle of arms and legs.

"Suuuuuuuuuuusssssssssssaaaaaaaaaaaaaannnnnnnnnnnnnn!" they roared.

"Gggggggggiiiiiiiiiiiiiirrrrrrrrrrrrrrrrrrrrrllllllllllllllllllllllsssss!" she roared back as she dropped her clipboard and pulled the group into a large hug.

Celia took the opportunity to hightail it out of there. She grabbed the straps of her duffle bag in both hands and hoisted it over her shoulder. She pointed herself towards the Hedgehog Path and forced her wobbly knees to march forward.

It was time to survey the best route out of here.

As the other girls ran shrieking into each others' arms, hugging and twirling each other around, Celia plopped her duffle bag onto a bed in her dorm, then calmly checked out the bike shed (no locks), and grabbed two granola bars, an apple, and two bottles of water from the Chow Lodge's snack table (provisions).

Just as she was heading back to her dorm, Celia noticed a girl standing alone by the Meet'n'Greet table. She had clear pink skin and knotted blond hair that rested just below her shoulder blades. Her un-scuffed sneakers were still firmly tied on her feet and she had a slightly dazed look in her eyes. Maybe it was the way her thumbs were jammed into the smallest pockets of her jean shorts, or that her gaze rested just above the treetops, but something about the girl seemed familiar. Celia walked over to her.

"First summer here?" she asked. The girl just nodded starring at the ground.

"From the city?" Celia asked. The girl nodded again.

"What part? Brooklyn or Manhattan?" Celia asked. The girl looked up at Celia, then frowned.

"*Albany,*" she scowled, and turned away.

Celia shrugged, and continued walking toward her dorm.

There were long shadows and wild noises coming from the trees and tall grass on either side of the path. The choir of crickets, cicadas, and tree frogs sounded like a sprinkler that was stuck hitting the side of a tree trunk. Although the whole place looked like the shady parts of the city parks that her mother warned her to stay away from, Celia didn't feel scared. Instead, she was pretty comfortable in nature. Every other summer she had visited her Gran in Jamaica where she would spend the whole day exploring the outdoors. The earthy smell of warm ferns, the million shades of green felt familiar and comforting, like something inside her chest was expanding back to where it should be.

She explored the network of tree-covered paths and passed a boathouse down by the lake. It had a hand-painted sign proclaiming it the Ducky Hut. She meandered past old clay tennis courts, a dance pavilion with fogged mirrors, a ropes course that for some reason gave her the creeps, and several cracked basketball courts. Down another path she came to the Nesting Grove, a cozy circle of twenty wooden dorms, each with a wooden porch and a single rocking chair. Then she found the Dorm Mothers' cabin, called the Hen Hutch, or the Hutch for short, and the main office, or Command Central, as they called it. Celia had a feeling that everything she'd passed, even if she hadn't noticed the hand-painted sign, also had another nickname according to the Glynwood nomenclature.

Camp Glynwood certainly wasn't the intimidating, pristine country club that Celia had imagined, but it also wasn't a dump. There was something Celia liked about its slightly run-down and overgrown appearance. It was loved and worn, which was something she could understand. It felt like her favorite Brooklyn Dodgers sweatshirt. The one she was wearing right now. It was a hand-me-up from her younger brother, Kyel.

Celia shook her head and looked around. She was thinking it was too bad she wouldn't be here tomorrow morning, when a loud gong rang out five times through the trees.

At the Meeting Rock, about a hundred or so girls gathered around a large granite boulder that jutted out from the grass like the top of an iceberg. The Dorm Mothers stood on top of the Meeting Rock as if it was a theater in the round. After a rousing welcome cheer, the Dorm Mothers sang the Rules Song in a comically dignified four-part harmony. The girls joined in shouting at certain points. It went like this:

Dorm Mothers: *Don't leave your dorm after lights-out.*
Girls echoed: *Lights-out!*
Dorm Mothers: *That's 9:30, without a doubt.*
Girls echoed: *Without a doubt!*
Dorm Mothers: *No food near your bunk,*
Girls: *unless you'd like to snuggle with a chipmunk.* (All yelled) *Or a SKUNK!*
Dorm Mothers: *No adult?*
Girls: *No swimmin'!*
Dorm Mothers: *No exceptions!*
Girls: *They're not kiddin'!*
Dorm Mothers: *No smoking, drinking, or druuuuuuugs...*
Girls: *Or you're going home without goodbye huuuuuuugs!*
Dorm Mothers: *And last but not least...*
Girls: *And last but not least...*
All Together: *And last but not leeeeeeeeeeast...* (It sped up here.)
   it's the fun and laughter
   we're mainly after,
   so without further delaaaaaaaaaaaaaaay,
   hug a Glynwood-Girl right away!

And with that, the girls erupted into shrieks of laughter as they hugged every breathing body they could reach. Celia's cheeks were smooshed against the hard skull of a younger, redheaded girl as a larger girl sitting behind them pulled them both into a bone-crushing bear hug.

After the whole camp meeting finished, the girls split into

smaller Gather Rounds grouped by their ages to introduce themselves. The Elevens met at the edge of the Great Swamp just where it began to slope toward the Lake. The Great Swamp had once been called the Great Lawn, but was renamed due to the large puddles that never seemed to dry up. The girls were instructed to say their names and give one interesting piece of information about their lives. Most of the girls already knew each other, so they cheered and made silly jokes as each girl stood up. Celia noticed that the other Elevens gave a rousing cheer to everyone, even the girls who would have been made fun of in her own school. For example, when this one tiny, shaking mouse of a girl stood up, the whole group of Elevens began chanting "Maybelline, the Zip-line Queen!" over and over until she smiled shyly and put her hands up for them to quiet down.

Soon it was Celia's turn. She stood up. The other Elevens gave her a hearty cheer even though they didn't know her name. Celia felt especially tall and gangly with all the averaged sized eleven-year-old girls sitting on the ground looking up at her. She put her hands into her back pockets, hoping it made her look casual and confident.

"My name is Celia," she said. "It's the same letters as Alice, just rearranged into a new order. My mother is a teacher and her favorite children's book is *Alice's Adventures in Wonderland* by Lewis Carroll. She used to read it to me a lot when I was little."

One of the girls raised two fingers in the air, the Gather Round signal for wanting to speak. It was the girl from the Meet'n'Greet table. Celia winced inside. Susan, who was facilitating the Elevens' Gather Round, snapped her fingers twice, indicating the girl could speak.

"How come your mother didn't just name you Alice, then?" she asked.

Celia shrugged her shoulders.

"Thank you, Celia," said Susan. "Now tell us one interesting thing about your life."

"I thought I just did," Celia said. One of the girls giggled. Celia wanted to sit down. No, she wanted to sink into the ground. She looked up at the sky, and rolled her eyeballs back a little, a trick she knew for fighting back tears.

Susan spoke in a kind voice. "You shared some extra information about your name. Now tell us something about your life."

Celia thought about her life for a moment, still staring at the sky. What could she really share with these girls?

That she and her brother Kyel should be visiting her Gran in Jamaica for the summer right now? Or that they weren't because Kyel had been missing for over three months? Or that all the grownups thought he was dead? Or that she was the only person who thought—no, just *knew*—that Kyel was still alive? Or that she would be running away later that night to find him?

Thinking about her plan to run away helped her focus. It sucked the moisture from her tear ducts and firmly clenched her trembling jaw. She felt the crumpled bus schedule in her pocket, and looked back down from the sky to the Gather Round. The girls all stared at her with wide eyes.

Celia decided to fall back on her usual.

"Both of my parents are from Jamaica," she said. The other girls "oooohed." One of them said, "Jah, mon," in a terrible Jamaican accent.

"I was born outside of Kingston," Celia continued, "but we moved to Brooklyn when I was less than a year old for my parents' work."

There. She felt better already. They could have a little piece of her to examine, but it wasn't anything real or important. Sure it was *true*. But that doesn't make it *real*.

"How come you don't have an accent?" one of the girls asked, without using the signal. Susan coughed a fake cough and showed the signal of two fingers in the air.

The girl made the signal. Susan smiled and snapped twice.

"How come you don't have an accent?" the girl asked again, in the same chipper voice.

"Because I've been in Brooklyn since before I could talk," Celia said squinting her eyes at the girl, feeling like the answer was pretty obvious.

"Thank you, Celia," said Susan nodding her head. "Jamaica. Very interesting, indeed." She looked like she was filing the information away somewhere important in her brain.

Celia plopped herself down on the grass and tried to tuck her long legs into each other like the other girls were doing.

It was the next girl's turn. She stood up and began talking. Celia looked down the sloping grassy hill to the Lake below. Dusk was approaching and the shadows were growing longer. Celia watched the tall grass at the edge of the Great Swamp with fascination as fireflies lit up and vanished in rhythmic rounds. All the voices around her faded away completely and Celia was left in a quiet, peaceful place where she didn't have to think, or worry about anything.

Suddenly, Celia noticed something hunched in the grass.

A pair of golden-yellow, almond-shaped eyes stared at her with razor-sharp fascination.

Seeing them felt like grabbing two fists of searing hot coals.

Celia's whole body jolted, and she slammed her elbow into the ribs of the girl sitting beside her.

"Ouch!" the girl yelped, bringing back all the people and noises of the summer evening.

"Sorry," Celia mumbled feeling her face flush with heat as all the other girls turned to stare at them.

Susan clapped three times, the signal for all eyes on her. She scanned the group with theatrically alert eyes, before she cleared her throat and motioned for the speaker to continue.

When Celia looked back into the tall grass of the meadow, there was nothing but the glow and fade of the fireflies.

2. Violet

"You're kind of spacey, aren't you?" a voice asked. Celia looked up to see a girl standing next to her. Celia hadn't noticed that the Gather Round was over. All the other girls were walking towards, or already inside, the Chow Lodge.

The girl who spoke was the one from Albany, who also happened to be the girl she had elbowed in the ribs. Now that she was standing closer, Celia could see that she had electric blue eyes, kind of like an Alaskan sled dog, and her cheeks and shoulders had lots of freckles. Her forehead had been sunburned since the morning, and her feet were now bare. She was just chomping down on the last bite of a hotdog.

"Not really," Celia answered. "I'm just focused on other things."

"I didn't mean it as a bad thing," the girl said. She stood with her hands on her hips, but not in an angry way. Sort of like this was the most comfortable way to stand. She studied Celia carefully.

"Sorry I was rude to you earlier at the Meet'n'Greet table," she said.

Celia shrugged.

"I was in a weird mood," the girl continued. "I'd just said goodbye to my mom, and it hadn't gone so well. Actually, we sort of had a little fight."

"About what?" Celia asked, her interest piquing.

"Oh, you know… abandoning her only daughter in the woods for the summer," the girl said, but a twinkle in the girl's eyes told Celia that she was actually poking fun of herself.

"Sorry I elbowed you," Celia said. "It was an accident."

"It's okay," said the girl. "I'll probably only be crippled for a short while." There was a brief moment of silence. Then she burst out laughing at her own joke. Her laugh made Celia think of a flash of tinsel catching the sunlight from a grey, winter sidewalk. There was a sharp crispness wrapped in sadness that Celia understood.

"My name is Violet," the girl said.

"I'm Celia."

"I know," Violet said. "I was listening at the Gather Round. Unlike you…"

"Oh, sorry," said Celia.

"It's alright. I'm not your teacher or anything. I was just wondering what you were thinking about, that's all."

"Oh, I don't know," Celia said. "I don't remember. Just being spacey, I guess." She faked her most convincing smile. Actually, she knew *exactly* what she had been thinking about – her plans for running away that night, finding Kyel, and wondering if she had finally cracked up, seeing things – those golden-yellow eyes.

"Your face looked pretty serious," Violet said. Then she made a super serious face. She crinkled her lips into a scowl and scrunched her eyebrows down so that they made tiny wrinkles on her forehead. Celia cracked a smile. Violet stopped making the face and smiled back.

"It's nice to see the sun finally come out," Violet said, referring to Celia's smile.

"Yeah, I guess," Celia said. She twisted her fingers into her

Dodgers sweatshirt and pulled the material taut.

"By the way," Violet added. "I'm the one who asked why your mom didn't just name you Alice."

Celia raised her eyebrow but didn't say anything. Violet continued talking.

"I wasn't trying to embarrass you or anything...it's just that I'm interested in why people get their names. Take my name, for example. Some people think that I was named after the precious, delicate, dainty flower Violet..." she did a little princess curtsey here, "but it's not true. I wasn't."

Violet took something out of the neck of her t-shirt and held it up to the sky like she was a superhero holding the key to the universe. Then she brought it back down to Celia's eye-level so she could see it. It was a small plastic prism threaded on a thin leather cord. The prism caught the setting rays of the sun and threw tiny rainbows across Celia's arms and face. Violet held the prism very still and then pointed to one of the rainbows.

"My father was a carpenter..."

"*Was?*"

"Was," Violet confirmed.

"Unemployed?"

"Dead."

"Oh," Celia said in a flat tone. She felt an instant tightening in her jaw, as she took a quick, shallow breath. "Sorry," she added.

"Well," Violet continued, "he *was* a carpenter by trade, but a physicist at heart. He was obsessed with everything there was to know about physics and light. My parents named me after ultraviolet rays. Ultraviolet wavelengths are shorter than visible light, but they are very powerful. They can disinfect water to make it safe for drinking, or mutate your cells and kill you with cancer. For good or for bad, they're super powerful. Our world wouldn't be the same without them."

She pointed to the colorless place next to violet on the rainbow and said, "If we could see them, they would be right here on the rainbow. But you can't. They are just beyond the visible spectrum."

Celia looked into Violet's crystal blue eyes. They flashed again with defiant ferocity.

"So, see – the reason for my name tells you something about me. Powerful ultraviolet rays, not some pitiful flower."

Celia said nothing.

Violet shrugged her shoulders.

"Well, anyway." She dropped the little prism into Celia's lap.

"You can borrow this…so you remember my name. And maybe it will help you remember why your mom named you Celia, instead of Alice."

"Um, okay," Celia said, holding the prism in her hand. She knew exactly why she was named Celia, instead of Alice, but that wasn't the point. She was done "sharing" personal information for the day.

"Aaaaaaaand," Violet jabbed a thumb toward the Chow Lodge. "You'd better grab your grub soon. It seems to me like food doesn't last long around here." She turned suddenly and dropped into a track sprinter's pose with both hands on the ground, one leg crouched beneath her, and the other leg extended behind her.

"I'm in Great Dorm 8 if you want to stop by during Free Choice. See you around Ce-Ce," she said. Then she yelled, "BANG!" and sprinted full speed toward one of the paths in the woods.

Celia stared after the streak of blonde that weaved around a larger group of girls also heading back to the dorms. No one had called her Ce-Ce in a while.

Now that the girl was gone, Celia's mind filled with tons of questions to ask her. She wanted to know how Violet's father died, and how old she had been when it happened. Maybe, Celia thought, that explained the thing that looked familiar about Violet as she stood at the Meet'n'Greet table; she was also missing someone special.

Something in Celia's chest twisted open and she thought about Kyel. She could picture Kyel introducing himself to Violet, using his kind way to correct people who mispronounced his name, *"Ky rhymes with sky, and el is like elle, the French word for she. Think Sky-elle and say Kyel."*

Kyel would appreciate Violet's explanation of things just beyond the visible spectrum. Celia pictured her brother's intense focus as he used binoculars to stare at the moon, or the time he wore an old welding helmet all day searching for solar flares on the sun. Celia turned the prism over in her hand. Little rainbows scattered across her arms and legs. She wrapped the leather cord around her wrist and tied it tightly.

As Celia stood to walk toward the Chow Lodge, she heard a rustling noise in the long grass behind her. She turned and saw a flash of golden-yellow eyes followed quickly by a swish of orange-red in the dark of the trees.

Celia rubbed away gathering moisture from her eyes, and looked again.

It was gone.

3. Escape Route

That night, Celia lay wide awake in Dorm Lucky Number 13. The simple wooden structure smelled like Home Depot's lumber section mixed with a potent dose of passion fruit shampoo. Four small beds rested in each corner of the room with a small shelf hanging above them. Initials and inside jokes from summers past tattooed the underneath of Celia's shelf as she stared up at it. Her three Dorm Sisters giggled and talked from their beds.

There was Samantha, a Latina from White Plains who announced to them that she would rather be at Ballet Camp; Kara, a brunette from Vermont, who was taller than Celia and said she grew up knowing more cows than people; and Jessie, an African-American girl who was also from Brooklyn. At first Celia was really excited to meet another girl from Brooklyn, but it turned out that Jessie had been coming to Camp Glynwood since she was seven and already had a ton of friends. She'd also never heard of Brownsville, the part of Brooklyn where Celia lived, so there was that too. But Celia didn't let it disappoint her. She hadn't planned on getting too attached to anyone in the first place.

After about another half hour of more excited chatter, her Dorm Sisters' breathing slowed and deepened as they fell asleep.

Celia tried to remain as still as possible inside her brand new red sleeping bag to keep it from making that irritating scratchy nylon noise as she pretended to sleep.

Ever since Kyel disappeared, nighttime had been a particularly difficult time for Celia. She didn't have asthma, but lately she'd begun to really feel sorry for people who did. When she tried to sleep it felt like there wasn't enough oxygen around her. Like the sheets were wrapping around her ankles and wrists, pressing into her chest and pushing away all the air. It was the feeling of reality beginning to seep in, like water under a locked cabin door in a sinking ship. At first she thought it was because she shared a bedroom with Kyel, a bunk bed even, and his empty top bunk seemed to press down on her from above. But after a week of trying to sleep on the living room couch, she realized that the same feeling persisted wherever she tried to rest.

If she was ever able to actually fall sleep, she was tortured by the same nightmares over and over. There was one where Kyel was on the edge of a tall building and the railing was broken but he didn't notice, and Celia kept screaming to warn him, but her voice wouldn't make a sound. Or another one where they were climbing a tree, and the branch breaks. She reaches to grab him and she grabs his sweatshirt—the black Brooklyn Dodgers sweatshirt she had now—but she can't close her hands, and the fabric keeps sliding through her fingers. Or another one where they were climbing up scaffolding on the side of a building, and the bars and planks keep separating and shifting, and she keeps moving planks around to get closer to him, but they get heavier and heavier and the wind is working against her, and he keeps getting farther and farther away until she can't hear him screaming for her anymore.

Sometimes one dream would just loop on repeat. Other nights she had all three of the dreams in a row, one right after another. This was what Celia was thinking about as she waited for the girls to fall asleep. Inside the dorm, wrapped inside the sleeping bag, the airlessness was the worst it had ever been. It felt like a tomb. A hot, damp tomb without enough oxygen. Celia focused on breathing.

Inhale. Exhale.

Inhale. Exhale.

Finally, when there hadn't been a movement or sigh from the other girls for over half an hour, Celia got out of bed and grabbed her messenger bag. She was fully dressed in Kyel's Dodgers sweatshirt and what she called her "life uniform"—cut-off jean shorts, a plain white V-neck t-shirt, and her red, slip-on Keds sneakers. This is what she always wore when she wasn't in her school uniform. Her mother bought large packs of the Hanes V-neck t-shirts. Celia never had to worry too much about what to wear, or ruining her clothes. When bleach and scrubbing couldn't remove the stains, they became cleaning rags for her mom. Celia liked keeping things simple.

Celia double-checked her messenger bag for the two granola bars, an apple and two bottles of water. Everything was ready. She opened the screen door carefully to keep it from making that creaky screen door sound. Then she crept outside, practically gasping for fresh air. She sat for a moment on the porch's rocking chair without rocking. She surveyed the grounds. The dorms, the Nesting Grove, and whatever she could see of the rest of the camp, were dark.

She held her head still and listened.

Not a single human sound. There were cicadas, crickets, tree frogs, and some night birds, but no whispers, talking or giggling.

Celia took a deep breath, and like a possessed sleepwalker, stood up from the rocking chair and walked down the porch steps. Without bothering to crouch, or look left or right, she walked straight across the Nesting Grove to the Hedgehog Path, and back across the Great Swamp, until she reached the bike shack.

She chose a dark green bike over a bright yellow or red one and quickly walked the bike down Camp Glynwood's dirt driveway. She lifted the bike's back tire from the ground to keep the gears from ticking. Her faded red Keds crunched the gravel, but at this point, there wasn't anyone around to hear. She was on the other side of camp from where everyone slept.

For some reason, she had the Rules Song stuck in her head. She began to hum it quietly as she walked. *Don't leave your dorm after lights-out! Lights-out! That's 9:30, without a doubt! Without a doubt!*

She couldn't help but smile. She never broke the rules. Generally, her family's code of honor was to always do the right thing. But her dad had told her that sometimes this code was more complicated than simply following the rules. He said sometimes you have to break the rules if they are wrong and you are actually doing the *right* thing by breaking them. He used Mahatma Gandhi, Susan B. Anthony, Nelson Mandela, and Martin Luther King Jr. as examples. *You have to use your heart and brain to feel out what is right*, he said.

Celia felt like this was one of those times. She wasn't going to give up on Kyel like everyone else had. She was going to break the rules, because it was the right thing to do. She was pretty sure, at least… sort of. And this was kind of exciting. She hadn't felt excitement, or much of anything besides anger and sadness, for months.

At Glynwood Lake Road, Celia swung herself up onto the bike, adjusted her bag over her shoulders like the bike messengers do in the city, and began pedaling at full speed. She was flying along the dirt roads now. She had about thirty minutes to get to the Greyhound station in Phoenicia to catch the 11:27 p.m. bus back to Manhattan.

In no time, she had turned on Lark's Way, and now she was turning onto Carpenter's Road. She looked at the time on her hand-me-down flip cell phone. She was going to make it.

She was getting hot, so she pushed back the sleeves on her sweatshirt. Still too hot. Celia coasted on the bike as she carefully peeled off the sweatshirt and slung it around her waist. Then, something caught the moonlight and flashed on her wrist. It was Violet's prism. Celia had forgotten about it. She had liked that girl. She would have to return the prism to her somehow. Maybe she could find the camp's address online and mail it back.

Celia returned her focus to the road ahead.

Suddenly, her breath froze into a block of ice in her throat.

A four-legged creature stood in the middle of the road in front of her. Its bright golden-yellow eyes stared at her.

Celia slammed on the brakes, but her body instantly became lighter than a whisper. She swerved the bike to avoid hitting the thing, but instead, the bike counter-balanced and veered straight toward it. She jerked the handlebars again in the opposite direction, but too sharply this time. She shot directly toward the side of the road.

Celia squeezed her eyes shut as the bike slammed into the metal guardrail.

Her stomach lurched as she flipped over the handlebars.

There was a brief airy lift, then Celia crash-landed. The bike slammed on top of her, because somehow she was still clinging to the handlebars.

The world kaleidoscoped into a jumbled confusion as Celia and the bike both tumbled down a steep embankment.

Celia on the bike. The bike on Celia.

Faster and faster. Out of control.

With everything clenched and banging, the taste of dirt and something metallic exploded into Celia's mouth – blood, probably.

She never felt the final blow of the tree that broke her fall.

Celia was already knocked out.

4. The Fog

When Celia woke up she was lying at the bottom of a steep embankment with the bike bent and useless on top of her. She sat up slowly, pushing the bike aside, and moved her limbs to check for breaks. The night was inky black, smeared with a thick fog. Her clothes and face were damp, but thankfully the moisture was condensation from the fog, not blood. She instinctively groped her fingers around to find her phone. It was smashed to pieces. The glass face looked like it was covered with the web of a frantic and disorganized spider. Celia threw it into the trees in frustration.

Celia realized her Dodgers sweatshirt was nowhere to be seen. She looked up the steep embankment toward the road. Nothing. No sweatshirt. No cars, no lights, no houses or gas station through the woods. Not a single sound or a single person anywhere. A chill ran through her body. The fog was twirling its way through the trees and around Celia. It was a silent, damp scarf wrapping around her head and ears. She had a fluffy, light feeling in her brain like her thoughts and memories were pieces of dust swirling around. She wanted to grasp them and arrange them, but she couldn't make them land.

Why was she here?

What had she seen on the road?

She tried to place the facts in an order that made sense to her, but they just kept swirling. She looked up at the road again just as it disappeared into the thick fog. Celia closed her eyes and then opened them again. She was wrapped in the fog, in complete silence. She reached her hand out.

The world ended at her fingertips.

And yet, she knew it didn't.

There was something else there.

She could feel it.

"Hello?" Celia whispered.

Without a breeze, the fog began to sway slowly.

"Hello?" she whispered again, louder this time. Maybe one of the girls from the camp had followed her. Maybe it was that girl Violet. She seemed like the curious type.

"I know you're there," Celia spoke louder, trying to conjure her bravery. "I know you can hear me," she said.

Slowly, at these words, golden-yellow, almond-shaped eyes began to shine through the fog. Celia instantly forgot about her aches and pains and began scrambling backward on her hands and feet. Silently, the glowing eyes hovered closer. Celia inhaled a sharp breath, ready to scream, when a full-grown red fox stepped out of the fog and sat down on its haunches in front of her. Celia's Dodgers sweatshirt rested at its paws.

Celia stared, still holding her breath, preparing to scream.

The fox was as big as a medium-sized dog. It stood absolutely still, staring at Celia, with only the slightest quiver in its ears as they honed in to gather information about her.

"Good evening," the fox suddenly said. Her voice was as smooth and low as water running over silk.

Then Celia released her scream. But the rush of air that came out

32

of her lungs was deflated and hollow from being held in for so long. The noise sounded more like a whimper.

The fox licked one of her black paws with a bright pink tongue, and delicately wiped the side of her orangey-red face. Then she wrapped its great bushy, white-tipped tail carefully around her paws and looked directly at Celia with eyes that flashed brilliantly.

"Wh-what?" Celia asked, not believing what she had just heard.

"I said, Good evening," she spoke again. The fox gave an exaggerated yawn and licked her bright pink tongue over sharp white teeth. Then she pushed the sweatshirt towards Celia.

Celia shook her head, not believing that she was speaking to an animal.

"Is it *not* a good evening?" the fox asked, looking slightly perplexed, and at the same time amused.

"What is going on?" Celia asked.

"You are a Speaker."

"A *what*?"

"A Speaker. You understand animals, and we understand you."

"I am not!" Celia stammered.

"But you can clearly hear me..." the fox retorted.

"Clearly..." said Celia, nodding in disbelief.

"Well, how delightfully rare!" the fox said giving a shy smile. "Please, I'm Tippit." The fox bowed forward and dipped her head to the ground. Then she nudged Celia's sweatshirt closer to her. Celia snatched it and quickly put it on. There was a tear in the sleeve, but Celia ignored it, managing to keep her eyes on the fox the whole time.

The animal was waiting for Celia to speak.

"I...I am Celia," she said.

"Enchanted," Tippit said, bowing her head slightly again. They both stared at each other carefully.

"I...have never spoken to a fox before," Celia said, not knowing what else to say. "Or any other animal," she added.

"I have never spoken to a Celia before, or any other human," Tippit said, "but since the moment you arrived at that human habitat, I could hear your voice, clear as a bell, ringing out over the usual nonsensical barking of humans. Speakers are so rare. I had to get a closer look. And then I thought, well, maybe we could talk. And well, this is fun, isn't it? It's just delightful!" Tippit looked very pleased.

Celia shook her head, trying to clear her swirling thoughts. "Wait," she said, the shock wearing off, "I'm sorry...how is this *happening*?" She stood up, and began pacing back and forth quickly.

"I was riding the bike, and then I crashed..."

Tippit watched her pacing, not moving a muscle but only her eyes, which were twinkling with amusement.

"Oh, I know," Celia continued. "I bumped my head, and I'm still asleep and I'm dreaming. Or maybe I'm awake but this is some strange hallucination. I just need to pinch myself and I'll wake up." She grabbed a huge hunk of her arm's flesh in her fingers and pinched. Hard.

The fox was still there.

Celia grabbed a different hunk of flesh and pinched harder.

Again.

And again.

"Ouch," Celia muttered and she began rubbing the raised welts that were forming on her arm.

A soft expression swept across the fox's face.

"Do not doubt yourself, Celia," Tippit said. "You are not

dreaming. You are a Speaker. It's very, very rare, but it does happen."

"But this has never happened to me before," Celia said. "I think I would've noticed talking animals before now."

"Well, as I have heard, it's usually just for a brief time. It doesn't last long," said Tippit.

"But why is it happening?"

"Why *not* should be your question," Tippit said. "You could ignore it, if you wish. It will go away, sooner rather than later. Or you can enjoy it while it lasts."

"Enjoy it?" Celia asked. Suddenly the fox sprang up and pranced delightfully in a little circle.

"It is a beautiful summer night and the woods are alive!" Tippit cried.

"Alive?" Celia said, thinking about Kyel, "But I was going somewhere important," she said, suddenly feeling a familiar pain in her chest, a feeling of falling away from everything pleasant and nice.

"Well, tell me all about it on the way," Tippit said cheerfully. "Wherever you were going could wait one more day. Being a Speaker could *end* tomorrow! I promise to bring you back to the other humans before daybreak."

"I don't know…" Celia said, looking into the fog in the direction of the road. "Maybe I should just head back now," she said.

"Well," Tippit snorted, a little insulted, "maybe you should. But that's up to you. I am leaving now. You may choose to follow me, or not." And with that the fox broke into a trot, and disappeared into the fog.

"Wait!" Celia yelled, but there was no reply.

Celia had two seconds to make up her mind. In those two seconds she thought about how she had already missed the last

Greyhound bus. She thought about the bike, crumpled and useless next to her. And finally she thought about Kyel.

She thought specifically about the way his determined, calculating eyes would squint as he invented the rules for a new game, the way he got that far-away-look just before he turned to her with a smile and said, "I have an idea...".

Then she didn't think about anything else at all. She tucked her bag behind her back, left the bike, and began running into the swirling fog where the orangey-red tail had just disappeared.

5. Tippit

Celia barreled blindly through the swirling fog, swatting low branches away from her face. She was one of the fastest runners in her whole grade, including the boys, but keeping up with the fox proved to be difficult. She saw the orangey-red tail disappear through the trees, into the tall grass of an open meadow. It sporadically dodged left and then right. Sometimes Celia almost caught up with the tail, but most of the time she just followed the sway in the grass, and the fog that rolled off it.

They reached the other side of the meadow and came again to thick woods. The fog was dissipating, but it was quickly replaced by a thick undergrowth of scraggly bushes, mountain laurel, and low-hanging tree branches knitted tightly together. The fox scampered under and around them, but Celia had to crash right through them to keep up. She created a loud commotion kicking up dried leaves and breaking through branches, but she didn't care. The only thing that mattered now was keeping up with the fox.

Suddenly, the ground dropped below her, and for the second time that night, Celia was rolling in a small landslide of soil and rocks down a steep hillside. Celia tried to tuck her body into a ball. She clenched her eyes shut from whatever was whipping at them. She felt the dull blows of rocks and branches on every part of her body, turning too quickly to know what to do, or to care.

Then she splashed to a sudden halt. Water filled her mouth, ears and nose. She gasped, and pulled her head above the muddy water of a small marsh. She quickly raised her messenger bag above her head to keep it from getting soaked. A bright moon had risen and it gave just enough light for Celia to see. The smell of frog eggs, skunk cabbage, and rotting leaves filled Celia's nostrils. She gagged as she wiped muck from her eyes.

She looked around and spotted the fox sitting with her tail curled around her perfect paws on the other side of a stepping-stone. Tippit was making a strange hissing, hiccupping sound. There was a hint of a smirk at the corner of her snout, which she quickly licked away with a bright pink tongue.

"Are you laughing at me?" Celia yelled. Tippit batted the question away with a flick of her long, graceful eyelashes.

"Are you alright?" Tippit asked.

"Delightful, fox," Celia replied curtly. "Never been better." She attempted to stand on her shaking legs, and fell back into the muddy, stagnant water. She tried a second time. Succeeding, she wiped a dead leaf from her face and flicked away a squirming tadpole that was caught between a braid and her neck.

The fox smiled, seemingly unaware of Celia's sarcasm. Her eyes momentarily darted to a bullfrog that had emerged from the mud next to the broad leaf of a skunk cabbage. Then she brought her attention back to Celia.

"I find it delightful to communicate with you, human child."

"Please call me Celia, not human child."

"If you call me Tippit, not fox," was the reply. Tippit looked at Celia without blinking.

"Alright, then. Where are we going, *Tippit*?" Celia asked.

"It's a surprise, *Celia*," Tippit said with a childish smirk.

"I don't like surprises," Celia said. Tippit squinted her eyes.

"Right now, we are going uphill," the fox said. She turned and began traversing a steep, rocky climb. "And don't even bother trying to argue with a stubborn fox," Tippit called over her shoulder. "You'll lose every time."

Looking around the dark unfamiliar woods, Celia followed Tippit without another moment wasted.

They continued moving through the woods and uphill the whole way. Celia shivered from being wet. She stopped once to wring out Kyel's Dodgers sweatshirt, but then quickly scrambled to catch up. She grabbed onto branches and rocks, sometimes pulling them out of the soft ground. Tippit looked back at her once or twice to make sure she was there, but always continued on without slowing. Celia was beginning to doubt the fun in this.

Eventually, the hill became too steep. The trees thinned out, and there was nothing for Celia to grab on to. Her lungs were burning. Her feet were heavy. She slowed to a walk. Celia watched as Tippit's tail disappeared over the crest of the next hill.

"FOX!" she yelled. "I mean...TIPPIT!" The animal was either too far ahead to hear or chose not to turn around. Either way, she was gone.

"Tippit?" she yelled again. Celia's voice echoed back to her, but there was no response. She was alone in the middle of the woods on an outcrop of moist rocks, slick with light green moss. The moon had moved behind a thick cloud and suddenly the night was very dark. Celia looked above her at the stars. She knew that some people could read the constellations like a GPS for nighttime navigation.

They guided many people in history through dark, dangerous woods and across treacherous oceans. Celia felt a pang of guilt and dismay that she didn't know the secrets of how they worked. She stood and looked at them. They were as useful to her as braille dots that a blind person couldn't reach.

"Tippit!" she yelled louder.

Again, no response.

She looked down the hill where she had come from. They had run so far, and made so many turns with no particular landmarks, Celia knew she couldn't find her way back to the meadow, let alone the road. The fog had blinded her for the first portion of the trip, and nothing would look familiar.

Celia sat down on the green lichen to steady her thinking. What *had* she been thinking? Just running into the woods? Chasing after a wild animal? For fun? She pinched herself again.

Nothing changed.

She was still sitting in the woods.

Alone.

Her thoughts were interrupted by a high-pitched *yip yip yip yip*. A snarling, grey and orange fuzz-ball rolled past her legs. It landed in the middle of the rocks and separated into two fuzz-balls, each rolled to a halt and became two small fox pups, or kits. They were perfect miniatures of Tippit, only their orange fur was tipped with gray, and they had slightly bushier tails and larger yellow eyes. Each sat up, shaking its head dizzily. After a moment, they spotted each other, and immediately charged again, choking and barking.

While Celia watched the blur of grayish-orange struggle against the rocks, a third kit had stealthily walked all the way to her and reached one of its small paws out to touch her leg. Celia shrieked and jumped to her feet, causing the small kit to scamper howling to the mouth of a den that Celia hadn't noticed before.

Tippit's head poked out of the den. She licked the whimpering kit as it rushed to her side.

The other two kits stopped their scrabbling to study Celia. They stared at her with golden-yellow, almond-shaped eyes that seemed somehow even larger than Tippit's. Then, without taking its eyes off her, one began to lick the other behind its ears.

"Everyone inside," Tippit said. The kits began to wail, resisting the command. Tippit snorted through her nose, and the kits scampered into the den.

Celia reluctantly approached the dark hole into which they had just disappeared.

"Everyone?" she asked, pointing to herself.

"Everyone," Tippit confirmed as she vanished.

Celia dropped to her hands and knees, which were already sore and beginning to bruise. She took a deep breath and closed her eyes. She saw Kyel's half-wink-half-smile as he looked at her and said, "Dare you..."

She swung her bag onto her back so that it didn't drag in the dark soil. Then she crouched on her stomach and pulled herself by her knees and elbows into the narrow, dark hole.

6. Tippit's Den

Celia crawled down the narrow tunnel, following the yipping and scrambling sounds of the kits ahead. After worming her way through about fifteen feet of the tight passage and bumping her head twice, sprinkling herself with cold earth, Celia reached a place where it opened up into a larger space.

The root and dirt ceiling was just high enough for Celia to kneel. There were piles of dried leaves mixed with loose fox fur and it smelled like warm animals and damp earth. The smell was strangely comforting to Celia, like her own pillow after she had used it awhile without changing the pillowcase.

Tippit remained by the mouth of the den. Celia's eyes adjusted to the darkness, but it was still very difficult to see anything at all.

"Pip, Layla, and Zah, this is Celia," said Tippit. They came forward and sat in front of Celia, studying her carefully. "She is a special human child called a Speaker. She can talk to us, and we can talk to her."

The three kits looked at her with rounded eyes.

"It's nice to meet you," Celia said to their bewildered faces.

"What does that mean?" Pip whispered to Tippit. This was the one that had been fighting with his sister Layla.

"It's something humans say to each other when they smell each other for the first time," Tippit explained.

"What does it *mean*, though?" Zah asked. He had been the quiet one who had touched her leg. Tippit looked at Celia for her answer. Celia thought for a second.

"Not much of anything, actually," Celia said, "Because humans say it even if we don't really like the person." The kits looked at each other, further perplexed.

"It's like giving someone a friendly lick," Celia said finally, trying to make it easier for them.

"Oh. Well, mice meat to you, too," Pip said. Celia thought about correcting Pip's misunderstanding, but looked at his little face, so eager to welcome her to their den, and decided against it. He trotted over to Celia and gave her bare leg a big lick. His tongue felt like wet sandpaper. Layla snickered and Zah buried himself in some dried leaves with a crinkle of embarrassment.

"Thanks," Celia said and gave Pip's head a gentle pat. His fur was surprisingly soft, like maybe it should belong to a baby chick instead.

"Can we play with her?" Layla asked, charging halfway toward Celia, perhaps a little jealous of all the attention her brother was receiving.

"Not tonight," Tippit said. Then she looked at Celia kindly, "but maybe the next time the Speaker visits."

The kits barked and bayed in protest, but Tippit licked them between the ears, making them drowsy and quiet. Pip's mouth opened into a huge yawn and his little tongue poked and curled exposing flashes of sharp teeth. Celia reached out to pet his round, furry, exposed belly.

"Wait here for a moment," Tippit said. Then she disappeared

down the tunnel. In a minute she returned with a freshly killed rabbit dangling limply from her jaws. The kits yipped and snapped excitedly as she laid the rabbit on the den floor. They rushed to the warm carcass and began ripping into its side. Celia winced, and turned away.

Tippit then nudged a half-eaten mouse toward Celia. Its little pink nose was smeared with blood, and its little neck dangled the wrong way. Celia politely declined and unwrapped a granola bar from her bag. It was completely pulverized into crumbs, but she hungrily ate the whole thing, and drank half a bottle of water.

"Auntie will be back before sunrise," Tippit said softly to the kits, but they didn't seem to hear. They were mitt-deep in the rabbit's side.

Tippit turned and motioned for Celia to follow her out of the den entrance while the kits were still occupied eating.

7. The Way Back

Outside, the moon had come out from behind the clouds again, illuminating the woods in a pale light that made it easier to see. They stood for a moment outside the den, Tippit listening to the kits, Celia allowing her eyes to adjust.

"You aren't the kits' mother?" Celia asked as they stood there.

Tippit shook her head. "They are my sister's children."

"Where's your sister?"

"She was killed one night on the road, not far from where your bike crashed."

"Oh," said Celia, stunned. She tried to think of something nice to say, but Tippit wasn't paying attention any longer. She was staring intensely at the ground, turning her head from side to side; listening carefully to something Celia couldn't hear.

Suddenly, Tippit pounced. There was an unforgiving crunch, and Celia cringed when she heard a poor creature's tiny screech of surprise and then the cracking of Tippit's jaw breaking through its little skull or backbone. Again, Tippit offered Celia the freshly killed rodent, but Celia politely declined. She looked away while Tippit sat crunching unceremoniously with a twitching tail and foot hanging out of her mouth. Then they began walking.

"Why did you bring me here? To the kits?" Celia asked. "You don't even know me."

Tippit walked awhile without speaking. Then she turned and looked at Celia. "I want to be your friend. And friends trust each other."

"Oh," was all Celia could think to say. They traveled awhile again without speaking. They headed mostly downhill, but sometimes across the crest of hills. Celia could tell they were going a different way from how they came, probably a more direct route back to camp.

"Where were you off to tonight, leaving the human habitat?" Tippit asked.

"It's sort of a complicated story," Celia said, hoping this would deter Tippit. Instead, it had the opposite effect on the curious fox.

"Well, then be sure to tell it from the very beginning," she said.

"Ummm... Okay," Celia replied. From the beginning, she thought. She took a deep breath of fresh air and held it in her lungs. She stepped over a large rock, moved around a fallen tree, exhaled, and then began.

"My mother is a teacher, and my father is a radiology technician."

"A radio-*what*?" Tippit interrupted.

"An x-ray guy. It means he takes pictures with a special camera that shows the insides of people."

"The insides?"

"Their bones and organs."

"Why would anyone want to see that?"

"To see if something is wrong – a broken bone or something."

"Oh," said Tippit, trying to make sense of this in her mind.

"After I was born," Celia continued, "they moved from Jamaica to the United States because the hospitals and schools pay better here. They also wanted me to grow up with more opportunity."

"Well, that's lovely," Tippit said, having absolutely no clue what opportunity was.

"Actually, the U.S. was very different from what they'd expected," Celia said. "Both my parents had grown up in the country, playing outside in coconut groves, swimming in the ocean, and running around streams and waterfalls. There were no fields, or woods for me to explore in Brownsville—where we live in Brooklyn—and some days the sidewalks and parks weren't even safe for playing. My parents were worried that I was going to be different because I didn't have those same things."

"And so," Tippit said butting in, as if fitting together the last pieces of a puzzle, "they sent you to the human habitat in the woods!"

"Not exactly," Celia said. She felt a familiar weight begin to tug on her heart. "Every summer they sent me and my brother Kyel back to Jamaica to stay with our Gran."

"Tell me about your brother," Tippit said.

Celia was quiet. For a while. But it didn't seem to bother Tippit. Maybe animals didn't mind long silences in conversations the way humans did. Celia stepped carefully from stone to stone to cross a swampy bog. When she reached the other side, she continued her story.

"Kyel was born when I was four. We were best friends from the day we met. Even before he could talk, we always understood each other perfectly. We did everything together. I know everyone loves their siblings and all…but we were actually best friends. Our teachers always let us spend our recesses together even though we were in different grades. We even had the same backpacks and lunch bags."

Celia unconsciously touched the strap of her messenger bag.

"Kyel wasn't just an ordinary little kid. He made everyone laugh, and remember what was good about stuff. He also made really cool things out of nothing. Our favorite thing to do was make mobiles."

"Mobiles?" Tippit asked. She was carefully balancing on a fallen log that crossed over a small ravine. Celia was walking below her, on the sloping forest floor.

"They're a kind of sculpture that hangs in the air, with objects that balance and dangle off of wires and string. We had one massive mobile in our room with tons of cool things that we collected in Brooklyn and Jamaica. It all started a few summers ago when Kyel found a tiny green coconut by Gran's house. He carved it into a little dinosaur, and made it the center weight. Then we just kept adding and adding things; old telephone wire, bottle caps, shells, sea glass, a lost earring from the sidewalk, and we created an entire little city dangling in the air. Anyway…" Celia caught herself getting sidetracked. "The point is, no matter what we did together, even homework, it was always fun and exciting."

"Just like when my sister and I were kits," said Tippit.

"Yeah," Celia said, "probably just like that." She grabbed onto a small branch as she passed a tree and yanked it. It broke and she let it fall to the forest floor.

Tippit could smell the change in Celia's breathing and emotions.

"What happened?" she asked softly, her ears lowering to her head. Celia didn't say anything else for a moment. She watched a spider scuttle along the crest of a rock.

"It was three months ago in early April. We had gone to look at the daffodils poking up from the dirty snow behind our school.

There is a stream back there—well, we call it a stream, but really it's some kind of man-made concrete u-shaped thing. Water flows through it sometimes, but other times there's none at all. But this day in April was warm and after a big rainstorm, and the stream was massive with melted snow and rainwater. It was swollen and roaring. Almost filled to the concrete brim. I remember thinking that it looked angry, but Kyel wasn't scared, so neither was I. We were making little stick boats and sending them into the rapids, a little flotilla Kyel called it, just a few feet away from a small bridge with a large drainage pipe." Celia stopped talking.

"And?" Tippit asked.

"I was focused on putting together a new boat, and when I turned around, he was gone."

"Gone?" Tippit asked.

"No splash. Nothing. Just gone."

Celia's knees felt weak. She stopped walking and sat down. She broke a small twig in half and began using it to dig a hole in the soft dirt. Tippit stopped beside her and watched her dig the hole with large, round eyes. Finally, Celia continued the story.

"Gran came from Jamaica to live with us for the rest of April and most of May. The police were so busy with my mom and dad, that someone had to take care of me. Everyone was trying to help, the detective, the minister, my principal—but..."

Celia worked harder at digging the hole with the stick.

"Did he come back?" Tippit asked.

"No."

Tippit was perfectly still, listening to everything Celia was and wasn't telling her.

"And then everyone just gave up," Celia said. "They just

stopped looking. After seven weeks, my Gran went back to Jamaica. My mother took the rest of the school year off from teaching, even though they made me go back to school. My mom put all of Kyel's belongings in boxes and packed them into the storage space of our apartment building's basement. Then she spent the rest of the time cleaning the apartment. She scrubbed it from floor to ceiling, and she cried big, silent tears while she did it. The apartment was very clean and very, very quiet after that."

Celia was digging the hole in the dirt so hard, her twig snapped. She threw the smaller end into the dark trees.

"My dad didn't talk much during that time, and he usually talks a lot. Instead he just hugged me more than usual, and he already hugged me a whole bunch to begin with. He would sit at the kitchen table and watch me do my homework. Then he would suddenly pull me into his big strong arms and hold me tightly, so tightly I could barely breathe. The warmth of his big heart would seep through my skin and I would feel my own heart begin to get warm. But then I thought about Kyel, and how everyone had given up on him, and it would go cold again."

Celia placed the other half of the stick in the hole. Then she used the little dirt pile to fill in the hole. She pressed the soil firmly with her fist.

"The third week in June my mother and father said they wanted me to go to summer camp in the woods instead of Jamaica."

"Camp?" Tippit interrupted.

"It's the human habitat in the woods," Celia explained. Tippit nodded.

"They'd used the money they'd saved up for Kyel and my plane tickets and put a non-refundable deposit down at the camp. They thought it would be better for me to spend some time somewhere new, with a bunch of girls my own age."

The night sky was beginning to turn a lighter shade of lavender. Brightness was gathering in the east; not yet a sunrise, but there were certain signs of dawn arriving. Celia stood up suddenly and began walking again. Tippit was now following her, instead of the other way around. Celia didn't know where she was going. She also didn't care.

"That's when I went from sad to mad," Celia said. "I hated everything: the silence in our apartment, and my parents for giving up. How could they send me away somewhere new? What if Kyel comes home and I'm not there? I decided that I needed to get back to Brooklyn on my own and start my own search for Kyel."

"And that was where you were going tonight?" asked Tippit.

"Yes," said Celia. They were walking side by side now. Tippit showed Celia the way with gentle nudges.

Suddenly, Tippit stopped walking. Just through the trees Celia could see all twenty of the dorms in the Nesting Grove, still silent in the dark. Celia looked over the quiet landscape. She felt like she had been gone for days, but realized it had only been about six hours. Tippit and Celia stared at the sleeping dorms for awhile.

"Celia," Tippit finally said, with a timid look in her eyes, "I am sorry that I kept you from finding your brother."

"That's okay," Celia said. "I'm not sure that my plan would have really worked anyway…" She looked away.

Tippit nodded her head silently.

"I would like to make it up to you by helping," Tippit said.

"How?" asked Celia, feeling doubtful. "The city is over a hundred miles from here."

"You are not the first Speaker who has come to these woods. There are other animals who... who are good at this kind of thing."

"I'm not sure," Celia said. "I still have the money for the bus ticket. I might not be here tomorrow night."

"It's your decision, but I will be waiting for you here tomorrow night, in this little clearing, just when the moon reaches the top of that pine tree." Tippit motioned to a towering pine tree that stood in the center of the Nesting Grove. "If you don't come... well, then you don't come."

Just then, a ray of pink sunlight broke through the trees and touched down on the dewy grass in the center of the Nesting Grove. A robin began to sing loudly on a branch above their heads.

Before Celia had a chance to say goodbye, Tippit looked at her, winked and quickly disappeared into the woods.

Celia watched the bushes sway until they were still again. Then she stepped cautiously out of the trees and into the clearing of the Nesting Grove.

8. Chow Lodge

Celia awoke from a sweaty haze of nightmares to the sound of the Time Gong ringing seven times. The booming noise ricocheted through the trees, across the camp, sending distressed birds flapping into the air.

"Do you always go to bed with your shoes on?" a girl's voice asked. Celia turned her head to see one of her Dorm Sisters, Samantha, the wiry Latina girl, standing in her PJs, staring at Celia's feet. She was balancing on one foot, stretching her other leg to her ear in some kind of ballet pose. She held a toothbrush in one hand and a bottle of hand sanitizer in the other. Celia squinted her eyes against the sunlight that was blaring right in her face. She mumbled something inaudible.

"Also," Samantha continued, "what's with the Dodgers sweatshirt?"

"I like them," Celia replied in a sarcastic tone.

"The Dodgers left Brooklyn and moved to L.A. in '57," Samantha said rolling her eyes. "Get with the times, and let them go."

Celia squinted her eyes shut, rolled over onto her stomach, and placed her pillow on top of her head. She wasn't letting anything go, she thought, and waited for Samantha to leave the dorm.

From under the pillow Celia considered everything that had happened the night before in the woods. She looked at her clothes that were covered in dirt and leaves. She felt beat up all over. It had been real, not a dream, and as crazy as it seemed, she wasn't surprised. Life without Kyel was the strangest thing she could imagine. Anything seemed possible now that Kyel was missing. If the sky turned green, Celia wouldn't think much of it at this point.

She heard the other girls yawning and stretching, then the sound of bare feet thumping onto the hollow wooden floors of the dorms. There were shrieks of laughter at the Sink n' Stink, as water was sprayed and toothbrushes were dropped, and the thunderous sounds of bare feet running across paths of firmly packed soil.

When the noises had subsided to a safe distance, Celia slowly dragged herself out of her sleeping bag. She peeled off her clothes from the night before and dressed in a fresh version of her "life uniform." She tied her sweatshirt around her waist.

The very slowest risers of the Glynwood Girls were already halfway to the Chow Lodge before Celia could even find her travel toothbrush in her gigantic duffle bag. She had noticed yesterday, and was reminded again right now, that most of the other girls had these cool stackable footlockers instead of duffle bags. Their footlockers were decorated with stickers and signed and cartooned with permanent markers. They also had handy separate compartments to keep things tidy, and slid easily under the beds, something Celia would have known if she had been going to camp since she was seven. Instead, she dug her hands around the jumbled contents of her massive duffle bag, searching blindly for toothpaste.

By the time Celia reached the Chow Lodge, all of the other girls were finished eating and outside on the Great Swamp sitting in small circles or running around playing an epic game of something or other. Celia pushed open the double screen doors to the Chow Lodge, and walked under a hand-painted sign that said, "This is where we Entrée!"

Only a single table of lingering Dorm Mothers remained inside. The two-story tall wooden structure was flooded with large columns of sunlight streaming in from gigantic windows in the ceiling rafters. A wonderful smoky smell permeated from a large stone fireplace in the center of the lodge. Celia followed its chimney up to the ceiling, and noticed a single random door up in the rafters. It had a small wooden platform in front of it, but no staircase or ladder leading up to it. Her attention shifted to a banner that read "Welcome to Camp Glynwood" hanging in the rafters. It was decorated with hundreds upon hundreds of overlapping handprints.

Aggie, the head cook, squinted at Celia and yelled over her shoulder, "Hold up! We got one more!" to someone in the back of the kitchen. They had already begun putting the food away. Aggie, who looked to be in her mid-forties, and of Irish descent, scooped together a steaming hot tray of scrambled eggs and hash browns for Celia.

"If you came through those doors thirty seconds later, this would have been one more portion for Rupert and George," Aggie said, chuckling. Rupert and George, or "the boys" as some of the Glynwood Girls lovingly called them, were Aggie's pigs. They lived behind the Chow Lodge in the Slop Shop where the girls dropped off their dirty trays when they were finished eating. Each dorm took turns washing trays for two days, six meals total, and "the boys" ate all the leftover food.

"Catsup is over by the juice, my dear," Aggie said.

"Do you have any hot sauce?" Celia asked. Aggie's eyes lit up.

"Well, we've got the regular Tabasco or Cholula, or..." she looked from left to right dramatically as if to make sure no one was listening, "Ooooorrrrrrrrrr... for the truly brave and culinary adventurous, we've got my own special concoction, Aggie's Taste-Bud Bruising n' Burning Brew, guaranteed to knock your socks off and leave them singed in the corner. How hot is too hot for you?"

Celia couldn't help but smile at this crazy woman's enthusiasm.

"Well, my family is Jamaican, so I can take a fair amount of heat," she said. Aggie jumped into the air and let out a loud yelp of joy. Then she did a little drum roll on the counter with her palms, and THWAP! She slammed a bottle of unmarked sauce onto the counter, and pushed it dramatically towards Celia.

"Alright, Caribbean," she said, "I'll need your honest feedback. You tell me what you think, and spare me the kid gloves. I plan to enter this stuff in a contest at the end of August, so I want the truth."

"Aggie! We gotta problem in here!" barked an older woman's voice from the back of the kitchen.

"Coming, Ma!" she yelled, rolling her eyes.

"Is that your mother?" Celia asked.

"No!" Aggie snorted at the thought. "Everyone just calls her Ma. She's the one who really runs this kitchen...she's a real peach, let me tell you!"

Aggie slapped the counter, winked at Celia, and turned to leave. Then she yelled over her shoulder. "Just leave the bottle on the counter when you're done with it. I'll get your opinion at lunch. And remember, nothing but the honest, ugly truth!"

Celia was wondering why the truth was always referred to as ugly, when she placed her tray on a table toward the front of the

Chow Lodge. The strong smell of coffee wafted her way from the table of Dorm Mothers as they hooted and hollered about something. She recognized a few of them from last night's Gather Rounds. There was Joanna, the ropes course instructor. She had short, purple hair, a nose ring and so far Celia hadn't seen her without her climbing harness on. Lisa was the one with long dreads, from Trinidad. She ran the Art Barn, and was the self-proclaimed Queen of Crafty, and not to be confused with Lee Sah, from Laos, who was the sports instructor. Celia also knew Shana, the tiny white woman with a shaved head, who was the absolute loudest of them all. She was the dance instructor from Chicago, and last night she had given a demonstration that had begun with classic ballet to Beethoven's Für Elise and quickly devolved into amazing dubstep. The woman popped and locked like Celia had never seen before. Even Samantha's jaw was left hanging open. Susan was also seated at the table, hunched over a steaming coffee mug, chatting with a few other Dorm Mothers that Celia still hadn't met.

Celia overheard Lee Sah saying that one of the bikes was missing this morning.

"Already?" Joanna asked, her carabineers clinked as she slapped the table. "Remember the kayak from last summer?" she added, and the table erupted into laughter. Then each woman joined in, offering her detail to the story.

Celia tuned out as the story progressed, getting louder and louder.

She dabbed a small drop of Aggie's hot sauce on a spoon and tasted it. It tingled Celia's tongue and warmed her belly. It was a delicious mixture of garlic, vinegar, piquin peppers, and chili. She poured a huge portion onto her eggs and took a large bite. What was that warm, smoky taste? She closed her eyes, and found the flavor in her memory.

It was her mother's kitchen on a cold winter day, the kind when the sun sets before you get home from school, and everyone is so cold and miserable from walking in the snow and slush. Celia and Kyel would come home from school, exhausted, and open up the front door of the apartment to the warm smell of spicy Oxtail stew simmering on the stovetop; the garlic and peppers, mixed with sweet cinnamon, ground cloves and nutmeg; the tender meat that falls right off the bone and practically melts in your mouth.

They would sit at the kitchen table, doing their homework, listening for their daddy to get home. Soon they would hear snow boots stomping down the apartment hallway. Then he would burst through the door with a smile as wide as the Atlantic Ocean between Brooklyn and Jamaica, taking a deep, deep breath in through his nose and sweeping up their mother tightly into his arms.

"You bring Jamaica right to us, my love," he would say with the bounce and roll of his island accent. And their embrace would warm the whole apartment, the whole block, in fact winter wasn't even outside the window any longer. Then they would sit around the dinner table, eating the delicious meal, all laughing and telling stories about their day; what Kyel brought to class to pass around at Show and Tell; what their Mama's best friend's niece said to her boss's wife; what Daddy's patient had written on his walking cane; which book Celia had decided to write about for her book report.

Celia was so comfortably plopped down in her memory and enjoying Aggie's hot sauce that she hadn't noticed Susan leave the table of Dorm Mothers and walk over to her.

"Mind if I sit down?" she asked. Celia jumped slightly in surprise, then mumbled "Sure," through a mouth full of eggs. Susan sat down and placed her clipboard on the table. She instinctively looked at something on the checklist. Then she thought otherwise, and flipped the clipboard over so that she couldn't see the list. She turned her attention to Celia.

"How's it going?" she asked, smiling.

"Fine, thank you. How are you?" Celia said feeling a little like a bug under a microscope, but trying to be a friendly bug at least.

"I'm great," Susan answered. "The first day and first night of camp were a little nerve-wracking," she unconsciously reached out and tapped her overturned clipboard, then realizing it, put her hands folded in her lap, "but things went off without a hitch, and today will be really, really fun." Celia was a little surprised by Susan's honesty. How could someone like Susan be nervous? Even if she was young-ish, she seemed so together, so in control. So clipboardy.

"How many years have you been here?" Celia asked.

"My grandmother started the camp in 1941, so, almost my whole life. First as a tag-along, then a camper, then as a Dorm Mother, and now as Director."

"Oh, that's nice," Celia said, giving Susan her most friendly and reassuring smile.

"This is my first summer as Director, though," Susan continued, "And to be honest, it's very different." She said the last part more to herself than to Celia.

"I bet," Celia said. And then didn't say anything else.

An eruption of laughter from the Dorm Mothers' table created a momentary silence between Celia and Susan as they turned to watch. One Mother slapped both her hands against the table, begging one of the other Mothers through tears of laughter to stop... stop...

just please stop telling the story. Celia caught something about a kayak being found wrapped in tin foil in the walk-in freezer.

"Celia," Susan began again, "I wanted to tell you, that I talked to your father on the phone yesterday evening."

"Oh, yeah?" Celia said, trying to sound casual, pushing her now lukewarm eggs around her tray.

"He told me about what happened to your family," Susan said. Celia stopped pushing the eggs. She didn't look at Susan, or anything. The world blurred a bit, and she focused only on breathing.

"Oh yeah?" she said again, this time with even less emotion. Susan took a deep breath.

"Celia, I'm so sorry for your loss," she said. "And I want you to know, that if you need anything..."

"My brother is not *a loss*," Celia said quietly, now staring at Susan.

"What's that?" Susan asked, leaning in to hear better.

"I don't know what my dad told you, but my brother is not *a loss*. He's just *missing*," Celia clarified.

Susan drummed her fingers once on the table, then flattened them out into a fan. "But your father said, that he...he drowned," she said.

"They don't know that," Celia said coldly, "No body, no proof." Susan looked at Celia with confusion.

"I thought that your father said..." Susan watched Celia's face carefully and allowed her voice to trail off.

"Listen," Celia said pushing her tray away, and looking directly at Susan, "I appreciate that you are trying to be nice, but honestly it's none of your business." Susan nodded quietly.

"You are right, Celia," she said finally, choosing her words very carefully. Celia was surprised by this. Susan continued. "I just wanted you to know that I am sorry…about whatever has happened…about your brother getting lost…and that if you ever want to talk about it…"

"I don't," Celia cut her off abruptly.

"Well, if you ever change your mind…"

"I won't," Celia cut her off again, but now Susan was determined to finish her sentence.

"… I am here for you," she said somewhat defiantly. They sat in silence for a moment.

"SUSAN!" Aggie's voice suddenly bellowed from the back of the kitchen, "we gotta problem here!"

"One second, Aggie!" Susan yelled back. She breathed in deeply, and smiled at Celia.

"SUSAN!" Aggie yelled again. Susan ignored her this time.

"Celia," she said, giving a heavy sigh, and flipped over her clipboard to inspect the contents on the list, "All the Glynwood Girls have their swimming tests and camp physical this morning. This afternoon you will choose your classes for First Rotation, which begins tomorrow."

Celia wondered if she would still be here tomorrow. She had to admit; Tippit's offer to help was beginning to sound tempting, and she sort of missed the fox's company. She thought about what she would do if she really did go back to the city. She would go to the stream, probably find nothing, and then what? Call her parents?

"Celia?"

"Yes?" she said, snapping back into the moment. Susan was looking at her with concern.

"As I just said, you should get your bathing suit on and meet in the Ducky Hut down by the lake in about fifteen minutes. The

Dorm Mothers will help you follow the flow of the day."

"Got it," Celia said, relieved that this interaction was almost over.

"SUSAN!" Aggie yelled. "The PILOT LIGHTS are out! NO STOVE equals NO LUNCH!"

"Alright, Aggie, COMING!" Susan yelled back. She looked at her watch, stood and gave Celia a friendly squeeze on the shoulder.

"Have a wonderful first full day of camp," she said. "I'll see you at the Gather Round this afternoon."

"Thanks," Celia mumbled as she stood to bring her uneaten, cold eggs to the Slop Shop.

9. A Bare Wrist

Celia was walking down to the Lake, adjusting the straps of her black Speedo one-piece bathing suit under her Dodgers sweatshirt, when Violet sprinted to her side and skidded to a stop on the wood chipped pathway.

"Did it work?" Violet asked. She was wearing a green two-piece bathing suit and hadn't noticed that her towel was trailing in the dirt.

"Did what work?" Celia asked.

"The prism! Did it help you remember why you're named Celia, not Alice?" A jolt ran through Celia's body. She pulled her sweatshirt sleeve back to find a bare wrist. No prism. Celia's heart sank. She must have lost it last night. Maybe it fell off when she crashed the bike. Or it could have been when she was crawling into the den.

"Ummmmm... not yet," Celia said.

"Where is it?" Violet asked, eyeing Celia's bare wrist.

"I left it in my dorm for safe keeping," Celia quickly lied before she could even think twice about telling the truth. Then she committed to the lie.

"I didn't want it to slip off or anything, in the Lake, when I was taking the swimming test," she said with a weak smile.

"Yeah, that would not be good," Violet said quietly, "... because I definitely want it back eventually. It's pretty important."

Celia thought about Violet's father and a knot began to form in her stomach. It was suddenly clear that the prism was from him. Celia didn't want to think about how she would feel if someone else lost her Dodgers sweatshirt.

"So, you just have it somewhere for safekeeping?" Violet asked.

"Yup," Celia said. "In my duffle bag." She messed with the hole ripped in her sweatshirt's sleeve.

"Well," said Violet in a cheerful voice again, "did you know that Jupiter has sixty-two confirmed moons?"

"No, but that's pretty random," Celia said.

"And awesome!" Violet said. "Also, have you heard why they call this Panther Pass?"

"Panther what?" Celia asked.

"The cut-through between Hedgehog Path and Toad Road? The trail we're walking on right now?"

"Uuuummmm, no. I haven't heard."

"They say," Violet started speaking in an unsteady, wavering voice, one that was supposed to sound spooky, "that many Glynwood Girls have seen the ghost of a terrifying Panther lurking in the dark trees and bushes of the pass!" Violet made a funny face as if she had fangs sticking out of her mouth and curled her fingers into huge claws and began to make growling noises.

Celia stared at her with a blank expression.

"Hey, Violet," she said, "I didn't sleep very well last night. I'm not really in a talking mood…" Violet dropped her hands, and covered her teeth again.

"Oh, yeah, sure… no problem." She thought for a second. "Are you in a walking quietly with a friend mood?" she asked with a hopeful smile.

"Yeah," Celia nodded, returning the smile. "That would be nice."

The two girls walked the rest of the way to the Ducky Hut to the sound of their flip-flops flopping and the birds twittering. Celia was happy to have Violet there, and Violet seemed happy being there. It wasn't an awkward silence, like it can be sometimes with other people. It was comfortable and natural.

When they reached the large crowd of Glynwood Girls and Dorm Mothers at the Lake, they were led in to separate areas according to their last names. A girl with red curly hair smiled and waved to Violet.

"Have a good morning, Ce-Ce!" Violet called to Celia. But Celia didn't hear her. She was already in her own line, staring at the dark water of the cold Lake. Girls were diving into the water, and swimming laps. Celia had always been the fastest swimmer on the YMCA swim team. The water had never bothered her before, but now she flinched at the sounds of the splashes exploding all around her. Celia pictured herself standing at the stream behind her school with Kyel. There had been no noise. Only the angry roar of the rushing water. That same roar seemed to be filling her ears now.

"Celia Johnson?" one of the Dorm Mothers yelled. It was Lee Sah, the sports instructor. Celia raised her hand.

"You're up!" Lee Sah yelled.

Celia snapped on her swimming cap, dropped her towel, and without another thought, charged down the wooden dock and dove into the water.

As soon as her face pierced the chilly Lake, Celia knew she wouldn't bother going back to the stream behind her school. There would be nothing else there for her to find. Celia screamed silent bubbles of air under the water, and barely felt a thing. She put her mind on blank-mode, and put all her anger and fear into moving her limbs as fast as humanly possible.

The swimming test itself was a piece of cake. She earned an "Orca" level, which was the highest level of independent swimmer. As she walked, dripping wet and shivering, up the hill to the Nurse's Station, she noticed there were only two other names next to "Orca" on the Levels Board in the Ducky Hut. Violet's was one of them.

***

The Nurse's Station, or the Cupcake as everyone called it, was a small round structure painted yellow that had a pink tin roof and resembled, well, a cupcake. It was located behind Command Central. Celia stood in a long line as Mrs. Nalgy, the camp nurse, had the girls file in one by one for their camp physical.

The only woman at Camp Glynwood to be called by her last name, Mrs. Nalgy was portly, and had been Camp Nurse for over thirty summers. She must have known Susan since she was a baby, Celia thought. She watched as Mrs. Nalgy bounced around the tiny interior of the Cupcake with the dexterity and joy of a chef at a five-star restaurant.

As Celia waited, she looked around the inside of the Cupcake, which was as organized as a submarine, with a place for everything, and everything in its place. There were medical supplies, books, tools, cots for sick campers, and a tiny living area with a bed, stove, and fridge for Mrs. Nalgy. A tennis racket hung above a small bookshelf of old Nancy Drew mystery novels, and Celia suddenly suspected that Mrs. Nalgy was an ace on the tennis court.

A poster of the human skeleton hung on the wall opposite to Celia. It reminded her of a family story she had heard told so many times while her mom graded papers, or as her father repainted a wall in their apartment a bright, tropical color. Celia stared at the poster, and found a particular bone in the knee.

When her mother had just graduated from college in Jamaica, her first teaching job was in a small one-room schoolhouse forty miles outside of Kingston. One morning she was up on a ladder, changing a light bulb, when she slipped and fell. Her principal brought her limping into the E.R., fearing a cracked kneecap. Celia's dad-to-be took her mom-to-be's x-rays, and although he was always polite and professional, he couldn't keep himself from telling her that she had 'the prettiest patella he had ever seen in his career.' A short year later they were married and Celia was born. A few months after that, they moved to the United States.

Celia stared at the left patella on the poster. That funny-looking, oval bone had been the beginning of it all.

"Celia Johnson?" Mrs. Nalgy called out.

"Present," she said automatically, jumping out of her story and into the current moment.

"Any aches, pains, digestive discomfort, or lightness in the head?"

"No," she lied. Actually, her entire body was aching from last night.

Mrs. Nalgy looked quickly with a tongue depressor down her throat, in her ears, and eyes...

"No tonsillitis, no ear infection, or wax build up, no pink eye..." she muttered to herself.

A quick glance at her head...

"Negative on the lice...beautiful braids my dear..." and then as an aside she asked, "Salon or mom?"

"Mom," Celia answered.

"Very nice."

"Thank you."

"Let's see…" Mrs. Nalgy went back to her more official sounding voice, "age is eleven. Menstruation started?"

"Yes," Celia answered.

"Any questions about that?"

"Nope," Celia said.

"Fabulous. Allergies? Asthma? Or anything else I should know?"

"No," Celia answered.

Mrs. Nalgy peered at Celia's health forms from her doctor back in Brooklyn. She rattled off Celia's parents' cell phone numbers.

"Correct?" she asked.

"Yup," Celia answered. Mrs. Nalgy looked at Celia and gave the whole child a quick study. Equally as satisfied with the sum of all the parts, she gave Celia a smile and shooed her out the door.

In no time at all, Celia was standing outside of the Cupcake, with a whole hour of free time before her.

"Celia!" yelled Jessie, her Dorm Sister, "Come play Snatch the Sneakers! It's like Capture the Flag but you have to capture the other teams' shoes off their feet."

Celia waved and smiled, but opted out. Samantha stood squinting at her.

"What? Too good to play with us, Brooklyn?" she yelled.

"Just tired," Celia replied, trying to ignore the sting in her Dorm Sister's tone. Samantha waved away this comment with a flip of her hip and her ponytail. Celia reconsidered for a moment, but then felt the drag in her tired muscles. She desperately needed a nap. She headed towards the quiet path and away from the rest of the girls.

The Nesting Grove was quiet and peaceful. She settled down onto her cot, struggling to find a position that didn't rest on one of her new aches or bruises. Just as she was about to fall asleep, she heard a voice whisper.

"There she is!" it squeaked. It was very close to her head, and Celia opened one eye, expecting to see a Dorm Sister staring at her, or maybe Samantha had come back for her. Instead she saw two chipmunks sitting on the wooden window ledge on the other side of the heavy screen.

"That's her?' the other asked, nibbling fastidiously on a tiny pinecone. They stared at her with darting, nervous eyes.

"How do you know?" the other one asked.

Just then the screen door slammed open and Kara, the overly tall brunette from Vermont walked in, placing a set of dripping goggles on the floor.

"Hey! Did you bring food into the dorm?" she asked eyeing the two chipmunks who still hadn't moved.

"No," Celia said, shaking her head, "I think they're just curious." As she spoke, the chipmunks' little eyes grew very large in their heads. With a burst of lightning speed, they scampered away into the brush behind the dorm.

"It's heeeeeerrrrrrrrrrrrrrrrrrrrrrrrrrrr!" they squealed.

Celia couldn't help but smile to herself as she turned over in bed to face the wall. *Let them spread the word all over the woods,* she thought. She had made up her mind to go back.

10. Anayla and Her Pack

That night, Celia lay anxiously in bed, listening to the peaceful breathing of her Dorm Sisters. Samantha was curled in a little ball at the top of her bed. Kara was on her side, slightly snoring, and Jessie was buried deep into her sleeping bag so that nothing was showing. The long day's fresh air and running around had them falling asleep a lot faster tonight. Even with her afternoon nap, Celia struggled a little to keep herself awake as she watched the moon rise in the sky. When it reached the top of the pine tree in the center of the Nesting Grove, she pulled her sleeping bag away. Fully dressed, she quietly opened the screen door and stepped out of the dorm.

Tippit was waiting for her in the small clearing exactly where they had planned. The fox nodded to Celia without a word and turned, slipping silently into the trees away from the sleeping camp. After they had walked through the woods for about fifteen minutes, Tippit turned and smiled.

"Welcome back," she said warmly. "I was worried you might not come."

"Actually, I've been looking forward to this all day," Celia said, and as she did, she realized it was true.

"Well, me too," Tippit said. She looked slightly bashful. "I also wanted to return this... is it yours?" she asked. She scraped away some leaves at the base of a tree to reveal Violet's prism on the leather cord.

"Yes!" Celia exclaimed, relieved to see it. She had avoided Violet at dinner and the S'mores Smoke-off, not wanting to have to complicate her lie even further.

"Layla found it outside our den this morning," Tippit said. "I had a very difficult time getting it away from her. Just a fair warning, she may be a little standoffish the next time you see her."

"Thank you!" Celia said, wrapping the cord around her wrist tightly and pulling it into a strong knot. "It belongs to my friend," she said, surprised at how nice it felt to call Violet a friend, "and it's very important to her." Celia felt so relieved to have the prism again, part of her wanted to run back to camp and give it to Violet now.

"Right, okay, well, speaking of important things," Tippit said, "we have someone to visit who I think can help you find Kyel." Any thoughts of returning to camp instantly vanished from Celia's mind.

"Who?" she asked.

"Oh, you will see when we get there," Tippit said, looking a little nervous, but also excited. "I think this will work," she said under her breath, mostly to herself.

"Think?" Celia said.

"Well… we'll have to see won't we?" Tippit began trotting ahead of Celia.

As they walked through the woods, Celia had time to look at the trees and rocks. She noticed a family of opossums hanging upside-down from a tree branch. Their little mouths hung open as they stared at Celia, listening to her voice.

Tippit and Celia were walking in a new direction, away from where they had traveled to the den. As the moon rose higher, shadows began to appear at the base of the trees. Celia noticed that Tippit had picked up her pace significantly. They moved without talking, and after a while the trees began to blur together. Celia let her mind begin to wander, and immediately she was running through the coconut groves with Kyel in Jamaica. They were climbing the tall slender trees, and running around with the other kids. They were breaking open coconuts and drinking their sweet water, which tasted nothing like the bottled kind you buy at the grocery store in Brooklyn that were all bitter and tangy. They were steering clear of stray dogs, collecting chicken eggs, maybe even chasing down a guinea hen that had gotten away. Guinea hens were good for eating bugs out of the vegetable garden, and also, according to her Gran, good at digging up things that someone might have buried in your yard to place a curse.

Suddenly, Celia tripped on a root, and caught herself on a large boulder. She shook the memories from her head. She was in the woods, in upstate New York, and she needed to pay attention so she didn't break her neck. Plus, it was sad to think of where she was and *wasn't*. Who she *wasn't* with. What would happen to all these memories if she never found Kyel? Where did they go? If it was something that only the two of them saw and knew, and he was truly gone, did the memories ever really happen?

Tippit paused to take a drink of fresh spring water dripping from an outcropping of rocks. Celia was contemplating trying the water herself, when a long, ragged howl—primal and true—echoed from deep in the woods.

Tippit froze.

The hair on Celia's arms stood up.

Tippit lifted her nose to the air and smelled deeply. The fur on the ruff of her neck stood up straight, but she had a strange lopsided smile on her face.

"Wolves," she whispered.

Something washed around the inside of Celia's chest. It was a feeling of cold, light air; the prickley feeling of fear.

"What do we do?" Celia asked. A second howl echoed through the woods. It was closer this time.

"Run! This is our chance to catch them!" Tippit answered.

"Catch them?" Celia yelled, but Tippit was already scampering away from her.

Celia scrambled after Tippit down the side of a small valley, moving so fast in leaps and bounds that her feet barely touched the ground. The ragged and spine-tingling howls came from all directions now, and soon there was panting and snorting between them.

As Tippit ran, she kept calling out with sharp, shrill barks. It was an unpleasant sound and Celia wished Tippit would stop.

The pack fanned out so that Celia could catch glimpses of the giant beasts, snapping their jowls, running beside them in the woods. There were two of them. Then four. Now six. Two ran past Tippit and Celia, and then slowed.

Tippit and Celia changed directions. There was only one more little crest before they reached the ridge that lead to the top of the mountain. But before they reached the ridge, Celia's foot caught in a small hole, and she toppled to the ground behind a large fallen tree. Tippit came skidding to a stop against a large rock cliff, looking back for Celia. Then five wolves skidded to a stop around the fox. Two more joined them. The dust and leaves cleared, revealing seven wolves fanned around Tippit in a semi-circle.

The wolves were huge grey monsters, at least three times the size of Tippit, with broad, powerful ribcages, and sloping backs. Their gray fur was peppered with black and yellow, except one of them who was pitch black. The wolves held their massive heads low, panting with their tongues hung out to the side, bearing sharp, yellowish-white teeth. Whining and yelping, they pawed the ground, piercing the silence with shrill barks of excitement.

Celia looked at the sheer rock face behind Tippit.

She was trapped. They had been led to this point, Celia thought. Driven.

Tippit crouched low to the ground, trembling slightly. Her ears were flat against her head, and her tail tucked beneath her body as she quietly looked past the wolves and scanned the woods for Celia.

Then the largest wolf, the black one, stepped forward toward Tippit. She held her head high above her erect body. Her muscles rippled under her shining fur as she moved closer and closer with her teeth bared and a stare fixed on Tippit. This one was clearly the leader.

Celia hunched smaller behind the fallen log. She was close enough that she could almost feel the beast's warm breath, and smell the dampness of the sweat on her fur. Tippit, however, stood her shaky ground.

"Brought yourself as a little sacrifice, Tippit?" the wolf growled. Her voice was gravelly and wavering, difficult for Celia to understand.

"Anayla," Tippit stammered, "that's not friendly…" but the wolf laughed and lunged. She snapped her powerful jaws. Tippit jumped backwards. The rest of the pack snarled and pawed the ground.

"Anayla!" Tippit yelled again quickly, her voice trying to remain calm. The wolves paced forward, closing the space between their heaving shoulders.

Suddenly, Anayla snarled and sprang forward, catching Tippit in her large, powerful jaws. Tippit yelped in surprise as Anayla's jaws clamped down on the orange-red scruff of her neck.

The frantic and hysterical sounds of Tippit and Anayla fighting boomed off the rock cliffs. Celia watched with horror as the other wolves whimpered and pawed the ground, foaming and drooling from their mouths. The air quickly soured from their sweat and breath.

With a quick flip of her smaller body, Tippit managed to scramble out from the weight of Anayla's body. The two beasts repositioned themselves and scuffled wildly again in the dirt. Anayla was much larger and immediately on top a second time. But this time Tippit lunged her full weight forward, and somehow she was on top of the massive black beast. They rolled in the dirt crashing into the circle of wolves surrounding them. Even if Tippit somehow managed to win this fight, Celia thought, there were six other wolves ready to take her on.

But then as quickly as it began, it stopped.

Anayla had Tippit pinned to the ground. Tippit whined pitifully from the weight of Anayla's front paws pressing down on her small chest. Her soft, white belly, vulnerable and exposed, rose and fell quickly as she panted. Anayla paused a moment to look at her pack. Celia was sure that the triumphant beast was about to use her razor-sharp fangs to rip Tippit's throat clean from her body. She crouched, frozen in terror, waiting for the final blow.

Instead, Anayla leaned down and gave Tippit's muzzle a big, friendly, slobbering lick, covering her face with snot and drool.

"Aghhhhh!" Tippit yelled, shaking her head from side to side, trying to sling Anayla's drool from her dainty snout. "Disgusting!

Anayla! Really, get off!"

Anayla and the other wolves broke into a bellowing chorus of laughter. Anayla stepped off Tippit and used her snout to give Tippit a friendly nudge to her feet.

"Not bad," Anayla said still panting, and working to catch her breath, "it took me twice as long to pin you this time."

Realizing that they had been playing, Celia snapped out of her catatonic state of fear. She stood up.

"That wasn't funny!" she yelled, her body still shaking.

Anayla froze. The pack of wolves whimpered and jumped back.

Not a creature moved in the silence that followed.

11. The Howling

Celia's knees became weak as all the wolves turned their intense stares toward her. She walked quickly to Tippit and helped her onto her paws.

"Are you okay?" she asked. Tippit gave her a feeble smile and a quick nod.

"A Speaker!" the whisper ricocheted through the pack. They whimpered, bowing and raising their heads. The pack, confused and needing direction, turned to Anayla. Anayla herself was momentarily disoriented and shaken. The hair on her back raised and her ears were perked and scanning for information.

"You understand us," Anayla said. Her voice was still thick and snarling, but now her eyes were soft and pensive. Celia nodded.

Slowly, Anayla regained her calm, dominant stance. She stood up tall, throwing her muscular shoulders back and expanding her broad chest.

"Forgive me, Speaker," she said. "It looks rough, but we animals were just playing."

"You were about to kill my friend," Celia said, still trembling a little.

"That's only how it appeared," Anayla said with a softness entering her eyes. "Wolves and foxes have a natural tolerance during time of plentiful food. My pack and Tippit…well, our tolerance had turned to more of a friendship. But that doesn't keep us from testing each other's strength when we meet. It keeps us all strong."

She bent her head and began licking one of her massive paws. There was a tiny trickle of blood between two of her claws where Tippit had managed to land a blow.

"Okay, okay," Tippit said, smiling meekly and stepping in between Anayla and Celia. "Enough of that. Anayla meet Celia, Celia meet Anayla. Celia is my Speaker friend," Tippit paused here to allow ample time for the wolves to be impressed. Then she continued with, "Mice meat to you both."

Tippit whispered to Anayla from the side of her snout, "It's a customary human greeting."

"Mice meat to you," Anayla replied, and the pack murmured it also, bowing their heads.

Not wanting to appear rude, Celia said, "Mice meat to everyone."

"We have not had a Speaker in these woods for a long time," Anayla said. "You must take her to the Feline," she added, looking directly at Tippit. The other wolves yipped in agreement.

"The *Feline*?" Tippit shuttered.

"That was what was done in the past," Anayla said, "according to our wolf elders."

"Perhaps…" Tippit said, looking unconvinced, "but I was hoping that maybe you could help her instead. Maybe we could avoid the whole Feline thing."

Tippit and Anayla exchanged glances. A silent understanding was shared.

"The Speaker has lost a member of her pack," Tippit said, "and I thought you might be able to help the girl find him, or talk to him."

"Is it true?" Anayla asked Celia.

"Yes. My younger brother is missing," Celia said.

"Is he dead or alive?" Anayla asked, looking directly at Celia. She paused, slightly taken aback by the abruptness of this question. The fuzziness returned momentarily, then rapidly faded.

"He is alive," Celia said, taking a deep breath. "Just missing."

Anayla's eyes narrowed as she stared at Celia, searching her quickly, examining every inch of her body. As she did, Anayla's ears turned to something else behind her as if her attention was somewhere far away, listening for answers. She raised her nose to the air and inhaled a long, deep breath, her nostrils searching to discover hidden truths. Then she bowed her head slightly and stepped backwards toward the pack. She exchanged glances and gestures with them, and Celia knew there was an entire conversation happening within those silent exchanges.

Anayla turned back around and looked at Tippit carefully, then at Celia.

"My pack will try to help you with your search," Anayla said, "But we can promise nothing."

"I understand," Celia said.

"We must return her to the human habitat before sunrise," Tippit chimed in.

Anayla nodded. "Then we should hurry. Celia, it would be my honor to carry you," she said in a soft, gravelly voice.

Celia climbed on Anayla's massive back. The pack formed a tight, protective circle around them and Tippit. As they began running through the woods, Celia could feel Anayla's ribs expanding and contracting beneath her. Celia had ridden a horse before, but that was choppy and bouncy. This was smooth and rhythmic. Celia moved herself away from Anayla's shoulder blades, which pointed sharply through her muscles, and leaned forward to wrap her arms around Anayla's neck to stay on. Unlike Tippit's soft fur, Anayla's fur was rough and bristly. It pricked against Celia's bare skin on her arms and legs, but she barely noticed this as they ran through the woods, leaping over streams, dodging trees and bounding from boulders.

The moon shone on the wolves' backs and glistened like silver. Their breath was hot and steaming. Sometimes they ran close and other times the circles widened so that they were only shadows running alongside each other in the trees. As they covered ground through the woods, Celia felt the presence of other creatures coming out of their warm holes and nests to watch them pass.

When they finally reached the edge of a clearing, the wolves and Tippit stopped together in a line. They stood in a small grassy clearing at the top of a steep hill where the moon shone brightly. The surrounding land spread out before them, like distant waves on a high sea. It felt like there was barely anything between them and the stars.

Celia slipped off Anayla's back and into the long soft grass. She faced the wolves.

"This is where we communicate with those in our pack who are elsewhere," Anayla explained. "Most who answer are still living, but some are not," she added.

Then Anayla raised her head to the moon and let out a mournful, haunting howl that boomed and lingered through each note. The sound was persistent and expansive. It burrowed into Celia's heart and lifted every hair on her arms, neck and head. The other wolves then lifted their heads as well and joined the howling. Tippit joined in with her own tiny barking and yipping howl.

The howling flung open a door inside Celia's chest that she had tried so hard to keep shut. Something great and large inside of Celia rose in her own throat, beating to break through to the surface. Maybe it was a great sob of exhaustion or despair, but whatever it was, she could not hold it in. She lifted her chin to the moon, and completely involuntarily, a long, lingering noise escaped her mouth. She opened her mouth wider, and released a pocket of concentrated sadness that she had locked deep in her chest. She sent the noise flying from her throat, into the sky and the moon with the other howls.

The wind picked up in large gusts that carried their sounds further. The howls echoed off the surrounding trees and ricocheted from distant hills and sheer rock cliffs, but then there was something else too. Celia listened carefully and heard new voices, other wolves and animals farther away, joining in and answering their calls. She could hear the volley back and forth between Anayla and other unseen wolves. She concentrated on the undulating sound, and then very quietly she thought she heard another human voice, one that didn't exactly match her own. Was it Kyel, miles and miles away, hearing her howl, and reaching out with his own voice to answer hers? Goosebumps rose all over her body as she continued to howl and listen. Again and again she called to him, and again and again someone, or something answered.

Then, suddenly, the howling stopped and the woods fell silent. The wind had stopped and everything was still. Celia quietly buried her face in her hands and took some deep breaths before she could bring herself to face the others.

"Did you hear a reply?" Anayla finally asked, searching Celia's face carefully with gentle eyes. Celia was surprised to see there were tears in Anayla's eyes. How could an animal as fierce and strong as Anayla cry?

"I...I think I heard Kyel answer me...but, I don't know," she said. "I heard something, I just don't know what it was." Anayla nodded, understanding. She lifted her head high and looked at the face of the moon. Then she turned to Tippit and spoke in a commanding voice.

"Bring the Speaker to the Feline," she said. Tippit just nodded and looked away.

"Can we go tonight?" Celia asked, feeling hopeful.

"It's too far," Tippit said. "There isn't time tonight. But we can go tomorrow night, if you insist."

Celia wondered what kind of animal would make Tippit shrink, when she was excited to see the wolves.

"I insist," Celia said.

"As do I," Anayla agreed. She seemed solemn and sad, but Tippit didn't seem to notice as she herself gave up with a sigh.

"Okay, tomorrow night I will bring Celia to the Feline."

After this was settled, Anayla and the wolves led them, in single file, along the ridge of the hill. As she walked, Celia kept looking behind her, checking to see if she was being followed. The unnerving sounds of the howls made her think of ghosts. She pictured a trail of the wolf ancestors' ghosts following behind them. Or maybe they were the shadows of every doubt she had ever carried with her in her life. Either way, Celia placed her hand on the scruff of Tippit's neck as they walked side by side, searching for comfort in her friend's warm fur.

At the far edge of the wolves' territory, Anayla and her pack stopped walking.

"We will listen to the wind for news of your search," Anayla said. "We wish you well." The wolves bowed to her. The muscles in their shoulders rippled as they touched their noses to the ground.

Celia bowed in return to Anayla and her pack. "Thank you," she said.

Celia and Tippit traveled silently the remainder of the way back to camp. Celia knew Tippit felt uneasy about going to this Feline, but she didn't want to discuss it. She kept hearing the sounds of the howls echoing in her head, and it was all she could think about.

What had she heard up on the hill? Was it just her own echoes? Or was it really Kyel? Maybe she wanted to hear Kyel so badly that she had simply imagined it. Maybe her mind heard something that wasn't there at all. Or maybe, just maybe, it was Kyel, calling out to her, trying to tell her where he was and how she could find him and bring him back to their family.

Now that this door of hope had flung open inside her chest, she felt more confused than ever.

When they reached the edge of the meadow by the camp, she turned and gave a quick hug to Tippit.

"See you tomorrow?" Celia asked. "Same time? Same place?" Tippit nodded, surprised by the hug.

Then Tippit winked, and said nothing. Celia winked back and watched her friend disappear into the woods.

12. Back at Camp

"Wowza! Did you hear those coyotes howling last night?" Susan asked the next morning as she caught up with Celia on the Chipmunk Run.

"Wolves," Celia muttered.

"What's that?" Susan asked cheerfully.

"I think they were wolves," Celia said. Susan gave Celia a sideways glance.

"Well, I guess it's possible...but I've never heard of wolves in these parts before." She paused for a second, and then continued. "You, ah...you feeling alright? You sound a little hoarse."

"I'm fine," Celia cleared her throat, which was actually pretty sore from all the howling the night before. "Just tired." At least the second part was true.

Susan smiled and placed her hand on Celia's shoulder. She looked like she was about to say something when they both spied Mrs. Nalgy scuttling toward them on the path. Her face was red and twisted, and she was muttering inaudibly to herself about a disastrous mystery. She lit up when she saw Susan.

"Susan!" she exclaimed, "A word in private, please?"

"Sure, Mrs. Nalgy," Susan grinned weakly, stepping away from Celia.

Because of their proximity, Celia couldn't help but overhear a part of their conversation.

"It's the rubbing alcohol again!" Mrs. Nalgy whispered in an agitated tone. "Three more bottles are gone!"

"Okay, Mrs. Nalgy," Susan said calmly. "When does the new supply come in?"

"It *doesn't!* That *was* the new supply!" Mrs. Nalgy said, exasperated. "This is only the third day of camp and that's seven bottles stolen! I'm going out of my mind! I don't understand how the culprit gets in or out. Or why!"

"Well, Lee Sah reported a missing bike, too. I'm sure there's an explanation for everything."

"Well, a missing bike isn't going to cause any health calamities…"

"All right, Mrs. Nalgy," Susan tried to soothe her with an even tone.

"I mean! I dragged my bed to the foot of the cabinet last night! I practically *slept* in the supply cabinet, and in the morning… Opened! Gone!" she was no longer whispering, but wailing in close hysterics.

"Alright, Mrs. Nalgy. I agree this is strange…"

"It's a mystery with potentially catastrophic consequences!"

"Well, I don't know about *that*…" said Susan.

"The culprit must be stopped. She…or he…is putting our girls in great peril! A simple scratch could now lead to tetanus!"

"I'll come by today to a put a padlock on the cabinet," said Susan, writing something on her clipboard, "Right after I order that new replacement part for Aggie's ovens."

"Tetanus! Do you know the pain and misery Tetanus causes? We are talking muscle spasms so powerful they can fracture bones! And all under my watch! Under my care! I can't even begin to imagine the horror…"

"Well, it sounds like you actually *have* begun to imagine the horror..." Susan said as she put her arm around Mrs. Nalgy's shoulder.

Mrs. Nalgy continued muttering and shaking her head as the two walked away across the Great Swamp towards the Cupcake.

It occurred to Celia how many moving parts existed in the camp. It was like a giant clock at the top of a bell tower. Most people only looked at the particular part that mattered to them, the clock face, while really there were tons of gears working all together behind the scenes. It was the same with Camp Glynwood. Everyone else just paid attention, enjoyed, or worried about the part that was important to them, but Susan had to think about every single moving part, and tend to them all at the same time. That was a lot of work, Celia thought. Why would anyone want that job?

Celia silently wished Susan good luck with her morning, and then continued walking alone down the Chipmunk Run to the Art Barn.

Today was the first day of Activity Rotations, and Celia was signed up for Sculpture Shop, Japanese Drumming, and Sailing. If she weren't so worn out from a sleepless night in the woods, she would actually be excited for the day. She had no idea that the activities would be so cool. A little bubble of excitement formed in her chest as she thought about learning to use a soldering iron, and manning her own little sailboat. She wanted to make a sculpture for her mother. Maybe just a tiny one to begin with. Something from Jamaica; a palm tree or a panga boat. That's what Kyel would do anyway.

While she was lost in thought, Celia heard a thunderous gallop approaching from behind. Without turning around she smiled and yelled out, "Violet!"

As if conjured from the clouds, Violet flew through the air, and landed in a karate kick-tumble-roll next to her.

"How did you *know*?" she asked, jumping up, panting and smiling.

"Lucky guess," Celia answered, pleased to see Violet's freckle-sprinkled smile.

"You have Batik Studio First Rotation, too?" Violet asked.

"Sculpture Shop," Celia answered. Violet groaned in fake pain.

"I wanted Sculpture Shop so badly," she said.

"Maybe you'll get it next Sign-Up Session," Celia said. The Glynwood Girls kept the same classes for three days straight. After that, they signed up for new classes and a new Rotation Period began. It was a pretty smart system, Celia thought.

"I hope so," Violet said. Then she drew a circle around her face with one finger, pulled her ears, and wiggled her elbows.

"What was that?" Celia asked.

"Oh, it's just my I *hope so* thing. You know how some people cross their hearts, or whatever. I do this instead."

"Okay," Celia said, stifling a laugh. "Can you show me again?" Violet drew a circle around her face with one finger, pulled her ears, and wiggled her elbows again.

Celia laughed out loud this time. "Thank you for sharing," she said.

"No problem," Violet said beaming. "Feel free to use my method any time. I think it actually works."

"I just might," Celia said as they came to the clearing in front of the Art Barn.

The Art Barn was a standard two-story traditional looking barn with nothing else traditional about it. Parts of the barn were covered in large mosaics that drifted into larger murals. Some even swirled into three-dimensional sculptures that hung off the side of the building. The rest was painted bright blue, and had curling yellow letters painted with arrows pointing to the different activities. There were multiple staircases that led to multiple rooms where different Dorm Mothers taught different classes. Sculpture Shop was around the corner on the first floor, while the Batik Studio was up a flight of stairs.

"Oh, Violet!" said Celia, suddenly remembering. She took the prism off her wrist and handed it to Violet, "Here you go."

Violet's whole body jolted when she saw it. She scooped it up in her hand and pressed it against her chest.

"Thank you, thank you, thank you!" she said. She did a funky little dance of triumph that ended with hugging Celia. Celia shrugged the hug away a little, but Violet didn't seem to notice. She put the prism around her neck and tied the leather cord tightly.

"I really thought for a second you had lost it," Violet said.

"Nope," said Celia. "Just keeping it safe."

"Thank you," Violet said again. "I didn't want to make you feel bad, but my dad gave it to me just before he died."

"Yeah, I sort of guessed that," Celia said. Celia thought about how nice Violet had been to her just moments ago, even though she wasn't sure if she would ever see the prism again. It's like she had already forgiven Celia, and put it behind them. Celia was twice as thankful that she was able to return the prism.

"Did it work?" Violet asked, interrupting Celia's thoughts.

"Huh?"

"Did it help you remember why your mom named you Celia, not Alice?"

"Oh, not really," Celia said.

"Shoot," Violet said staring at the prism. "I was hoping it would," she said.

The two girls stood in silence while a group of four Elevens and a few Twelves passed them, and headed into the Art Barn through different entrances. Samantha was one of those girls. She passed Celia without a glance or saying a word. Celia looked away, pretending not to notice. After they had disappeared, Celia turned back to Violet.

"Ummm, Violet, I wanted to ask you…" Celia said.

"Yes?"

"How did your father die?"

Violet gave her a soft, sideways glance, with a struggling smile.

"Lung cancer," she said.

"Oh." Celia paused and wondered if it was rude to ask if he had smoked cigarettes. She decided not to. It didn't change the fact that he had died. "When did it happen?" she asked instead.

"Almost two years ago, on the third day of fourth grade."

"Wow," Celia said quietly. "I'm really sorry."

"Thanks," said Violet softly. "Me, too."

"Do you have any brothers or sisters?" Celia asked.

"Nope. It's just me and my mom now," Violet said. They stood silently for a minute. Then the Time Gong sounded off through the woods, telling all the girls that the First Activity had officially begun.

"Well, we should probably get going," Violet said, making no indication that she was actually leaving.

"Can I tell you something?" Celia asked quietly.

"Sure," Violet replied.

"My brother, Kyel…he might be dead also," Celia said. There

was a pause as Violet squinted her eyes, and tilted her head to the side, as if to see Celia from a clearer vantage point.

"*Might?*" Violet asked. She sounded surprised and doubtful, which in turn made Celia feel surprised and doubtful.

"What do you mean, *might?*" Violet asked.

"I'm not sure if he is, or not," Celia said. She instantly regretted saying anything at all. She kicked her foot at a clump of grass on the ground.

"How could you be unsure?" Violet asked.

"Some people think he drowned, but I don't," Celia said.

"But…Celia," Violet said slowly, "it's not about what you *think*. It's about what really happened."

Celia shrugged her shoulders.

"So what really happened?" Violet asked with true concern in her eyes. Celia shrugged her shoulders again.

"LET'S GO, LADIES!" Lisa, the Dorm Mother who called herself Queen of Crafty, suddenly shouted from a window in the second story of the Art Barn. "First Activities have started! You'll miss introductions and instructions!"

Violet looked carefully at Celia, but Celia didn't say anything else. She gave Violet a silent half-shrug, half-wave and ran around the side of the barn where the bright yellow arrow pointed to "Sculpture Shop."

Violet watched Celia disappear. Then she launched herself up the Art Barn stairs three at a time to where the bright yellow arrow pointed to "Batik Studio." On the top step of the staircase, she stopped and gave her prism a small kiss.

Then she looked up at the sky and whispered, "Thanks for helping Celia find it, Dad. Might need you again soon, so stand by."

13. The Mountain Ridge

Celia's breath caught in her throat as she and Tippit stood at the top of a mountain ridge. Above them, the sky was a deep plum color. Below them, there was nothing but tiny green trees cascading down for miles and miles on either side. The air smelled like crisp, fresh pine. The wind picked up and rushed across Celia's skin and through her braids. Far away in the distance, the Lake glistened like a tiny gem reflected in the bright moonlight and infinite white stars above. They had run for over two hours to reach this place. Celia could have howled to her heart's content, and no human ears would have been close enough to hear.

Celia stood with her hand on Tippit's neck. Tippit sat with her tail daintily wrapped around her paws. At first it had been Tippit who didn't want to bring Celia here, but during their hours apart, Tippit's mood had softened as she realized that the Feline might be the only animal that could actually help Celia. Celia, on the other hand, felt the opposite. She had been feeling really strange and off balance since her conversation with Violet. She wasn't sure that she wanted to meet the Feline, or talk to anyone else about Kyel. She pulled her hand away from Tippit's fur and ran her fingers through her braids, some of which were beginning to loosen into a puffier form.

"I think we should turn around," Celia said, impatient and anxious with an itching feeling of uncertainty.

"We came all the way here," Tippit said, "Why would we leave now?"

"I'm just not sure anymore," Celia said. "Maybe we should just go play with the kits."

Tippit ignored her.

"Just go straight through there," Tippit motioned with her nose ahead through a gathering of strange rock formations.

"You aren't coming?" Celia asked, alarmed.

"No, Celia. The Feline would not wish to speak to me, and I would not risk my life to displease him."

Celia stood staring at Tippit with her jaw dropped open.

"Is he dangerous?" Celia asked.

"Oh, very!" said Tippit.

"Well, what if he attacks me, or kills me?" Celia asked.

"I don't think Anayla would suggest something that would get you killed," Tippit replied.

"You certainly place a lot of trust in an alpha-she-wolf that almost ripped your throat out," said Celia.

"But I *do* trust Anayla," Tippit answered.

"Well animal-trust, and human-trust must be two completely different things!" Celia practically shouted. Tippit and Celia both were surprised by the edge in her voice. Celia took a step back from the mountain ridge. She wasn't even sure what she was talking about. She was confused, and feeling forced into something. She hated that feeling. But she also knew Tippit was just trying to help.

"Sorry," she mumbled.

"It's for Kyel," Tippit said quietly, "and for you."

Celia put her hand back on the fox's neck and ruffled her fur.

"Alright, *fox*," Celia said, giving in. "Where do I go?" Tippit looked pleased.

"Well, *human*," Tippit replied, teasing her, "walk straight ahead on this path, and you will find the cave's entrance."

"Then what?" Celia asked. "Do I just saunter right in?"

"Heavens, no!" Tippit chortled. "Wait for the Feline to welcome you in."

"How do I make myself known? A secret whistle or something?" Tippit snickered and shook her head.

"Oh, Celia," she said, "The Feline already knows we are here. He could smell us from half a mile away. He is probably listening to our conversation right now. Just go forward and wait for a welcome. But do *not* enter the cave otherwise! If he is resting, you would not want to surprise him from sleep. Speaker or not, you would not survive that misfortune."

Celia took a deep breath. The insides of her knees were beginning to bruise from knocking into each other, but she knew she had to continue.

Without a word, Celia threw her arms around Tippit's neck in a big hug. But this time, instead of simply enduring the hug, Tippit nuzzled into the crook of Celia's elbow and licked her bare arm.

14. The Feline

The wind pushed past Celia as she walked through the large rock formations. It whistled and moaned, faded away and came back again. The tall rock gatherings looked and sounded like a shrouded funeral procession; petrified in its own mourning. Even though parts of the way were very narrow, Celia was careful not to touch the rocks. She was frightened to discover how cold the stone might feel, or even creepier, how warm.

Moon shadows grew along the ground at her feet and connected in pools of darkness. Celia moved quickly past the strange rock formations and through some short, scraggly bushes to a clearing where there was a large, unmistakable mouth of a cave.

Her heart began to race as she looked at the dark, yawning opening in the rocks. Although there was still some faint starlight from above, the cave was a total absence of light. Just like the black holes in outer space she had read about, the cave seemed to gulp up all the surrounding light. Celia walked as close to the cave as she dared, then stood silently, waiting, as Tippit had instructed. The wind slowly died down. Other than the shivers dancing across Celia's skin, all was still.

"Hello, human," rumbled a low voice from inside the dark cave. It was loud and sudden, like a startling clap of thunder on a sunny day.

"H-hello," Celia stammered back.

"Come in," it purred.

Celia took a deep breath and walked forward into the mouth of the cave. The entrance to this cave was made of large, jagged rocks. Unlike Tippit's den, where she had to crawl on her stomach, Celia barely had to duck her head as she entered the darkness. She reached both hands out in front of her and moved them about to keep from walking into anything, but there was nothing to touch.

Inside the cave, the air was very cold, but dry, and smelled like tree sap and something living. Celia stopped walking and stood in total blindness. The fear of something else in there with her made her breath rapid and shallow.

Instantly, she wanted to leave. She could see the newspaper headlines now, hovering above her head.

Girl Missing in Woods. Body Never Found.

The thought of how it would affect her parents sent her mind reeling, shocked by her own carelessness. Playing with a fox was one thing, running with wolves was another, but this...entering into a dark cave hidden deep in the woods to see an animal that unnerved foxes and wolves... was something entirely different. Foolish and hubris were the words that came to mind.

"Do come closer," the voice spoke.

Celia's hands trembled as she held them out again and walked, slowly and shaking, further into the cave. What little light the stars provided outside quickly disappeared. When Celia looked ahead she could see absolutely nothing at all.

"Stop there," the voice ordered. "Let me look at you."

Celia tried to turn her body to face the voice, but it was impossible to tell which direction it was coming from. There was a long exhale, a deep rumbling noise, that made Celia's shirt ripple.

Then, silence; the kind of silence that comes when someone is looking and thinking.

"I...I am Celia," she said, trying to be brave, or at least make whatever was going to happen next, happen sooner, so that she didn't have to endure the painful wait.

"I already know, Celia..." the voice said, turning her name over on its tongue, "You are a Speaker from an unlikely place. And your brother, Kyel, is gone."

"He is missing," Celia said quietly.

"Sit, Celia, and breathe," the voice said. Celia realized that she had been holding her breath. She let her knees fold and quickly sank to the cold ground. She hugged them to her chest and focused on breathing.

Inhale. Exhale.

Inhale. Exhale.

Slowly, the clouds covering the moon shifted in the sky, and a weak ray of moonlight shone into the cave. Celia's eyes adjusted to the light. She noticed hundreds of oblong-shaped objects that caught the dim light.

Inhale. Exhale.

She opened her eyes wider to see what they were. Skulls. And bones. Skulls and bones of all sizes, stacked in large piles against the rocks. Skulls and bones of deer, rabbits, fox, coyotes, raccoons, squirrels, mice, maybe even fish.

Inhale. Exhale.

Inhale. Exhale.

"Can you see me?" the voice rumbled.

"No," Celia answered quietly.

"Look closer."

She opened her eyes wider to allow as much light in as possible.

Slowly, she made out a large animal, much larger than Tippit, reclined on a ledge in the rock. Then the shadow grew as it swiftly lifted itself onto four legs. Like light moving along the side of the cave, or perhaps the absence of it, it slunk around the craggily contour and came to stand in front of Celia.

"Can you see me now?" he asked.

She could.

The animal was something Celia had never seen before. Not in books, not in zoos. He was a feline all right, but one that was larger than Anayla. His broad shoulders and muscular back were covered in dense, silvery-brown fur, almost as thick as a bear's. The fur on his chin split into a double-pointed beard, and his wide, erect ears were tipped with long tufts of fur, which would have almost been endearing, if it weren't for his intense hazel eyes that bore into Celia with deadly fascination.

"Y-yes," she stammered, "I see you."

The creature looked at her carefully, studying her silently for what felt like an eternity. Then he stretched his long, muscular legs and shook the sleep from his wide, padded paws, exhibiting thick, unsheathed claws.

"You are frightened," he casually observed.

"Yes."

"Not everything that is terrifying will hurt you," he said, and slumped down in lofty repose, a small distance from Celia.

Celia didn't know how to respond, so she concentrated on forcing herself to stare at the creature and calm her shaking. His nostrils breathed heavily and the two sat silently looking at each other for awhile.

After fifteen or twenty minutes of silence, it occurred to Celia that she would be dead by now if the Feline wanted to kill her. Once she convinced herself of this, she felt her breath truly slow and deepen. As they looked at each other, Celia felt a calmness slowly wash over her. She wasn't as frightened anymore. Slowly, she felt her curiosity grow.

"What kind of animal are you?" Celia asked.

"What do you think?" came his reply.

Celia's mind raced back to what she had learned in science class and from her own animal books at home.

"A bobcat?" she asked, doubtfully.

The animal scoffed, as if sneezing on some flower pollen.

"Oh, Celia," he said with a sigh, "your species' ignorance is staggering." Celia felt her cheeks flush.

"Well, what... what are you, then?" she asked.

"But, your curiosity makes you easy to forgive," the Feline added with a gentle smile that exposed a set of terrifying fangs.

"Humans call me a *lynx canadensis*. A Canadian Lynx." He shook his powerful head and the thick, shaggy fur rippled up and down his back. "You can call me Lynx, but I don't call myself anything," he continued, "I am simply myself. And the other animals, well, they generally stay away. If they can." Celia glanced around the cave at the piles of skulls and bones and understood why.

"They call you the Feline," Celia said.

"And they call you the Speaker. Is that how you know yourself?"

Silence settled in the cave again as Celia and the Lynx studied each other, each with their private thoughts.

"What do you know about Speakers?" Celia finally asked, feeling braver now.

"I know that long ago, there was another Speaker in these woods," the Lynx answered.

"Did you meet her…or him?" Celia asked.

"No. She came to these woods almost ninety summers ago. Very few of the animals alive today had been born yet, myself included. We have heard stories and rumors about her from older generations."

"So it was another girl?" Celia asked.

"Not a girl. A young woman. She was older than you when she was able to Speak. My mother told me the Speaker was in her twentieth summer."

"Did your mother meet her?" Celia asked.

"My mother knew the Speaker very well. They were special companions. Perhaps similar to you and the fox…"

"Tippit," Celia said.

"Yes," the Lynx continued, "My mother and the Speaker spent the whole summer together, walking these woods and mountain ridges, talking."

"Did the Speaker live with your mother?"

"No. She lived alone in a habitat by the Lake. The wolves, Anayla's mothers and grandmothers, would bring her to this cave. Or sometimes my mother would go down the mountain to the Speaker." Celia thought about this. Now it makes sense why Anayla insisted that Celia go to the Lynx. It was probably what she had been told by her parents and grandparents.

"Did your mother ever tell you what they talked about?" Celia asked.

"She only said that it was a summer filled with joy and loss. They roamed and explored the woods, laughing and talking, but the

Speaker's father had just died, and oftentimes she talked of being lost and very lonely. But no matter, my mother said they enjoyed their time together right up until the very end."

"And how did their time together end?" Celia asked. She hadn't given much thought yet as to how and when the powers of Speaking might wear off.

The Lynx sighed heavily and rolled onto his back. He scratched his massive shoulders and spine from side to side against the cave's rough floor. Then he flipped back onto his stomach, twitching his fur all the while to flick off the dust and jagged pebbles.

"Unfortunately," he explained, "this is the part that we animals understand the least. The way the older generation told it, the summer ended with confusion that caused great mistrust between certain animals."

"Like what?"

As the Lynx began to speak again, the very tip of his tail swished from side to side in an expression of vexation, rather than playfulness.

"The very last time my mother saw the Speaker they met by the Lake. When she found the Speaker, the young woman was crying and carrying a dead Snapping Turtle in her arms. When the Speaker tried to explain to my mother what had happened, her words were meaningless noises. They could no longer Speak. The garbled barking noises of the human scared my mother, and the snarling hissing noises of my mother scared the human. The Speaker, who was no longer a Speaker, ran to her habitat still holding the Snapping Turtle's dead body. My mother retreated back up to the mountaintop, and never learned what had taken place. The two never saw each other again."

The Lynx interrupted his story here to lick one of his massive paws and then wipe the side of his face. Then he continued.

"It didn't take long for the news to reach the other Snapping Turtles. They came to the edge of the Lake, and smelled the death of one of their kind in the air. They saw the Speaker and my mother's footprints in the mud. Ever since then, they have blamed humans and Lynxes for the Snapping Turtle's death."

"And your mother never saw the Speaker again?" Celia asked.

"Many years later, when she was very old and beginning to lose her senses, my mother would sometimes stumble down the mountain to the human habitat, looking for her friend. She never found the Speaker again, although I do think she may have given some younger humans quite a scare." Celia couldn't help but think about the rumors behind Panther Pass.

"So your mother never found out what happened to the Snapping Turtle?"

"No, but it makes no difference to the Snapping Turtle King," the Lynx said.

"The *Snapping Turtle King*?" Celia repeated. The name sent a chill rippling across her heart. The Lynx nodded, silently.

"The turtle that the Speaker carried away wasn't just any turtle," he explained, "She was the Snapping Turtle Queen."

Celia felt uneasy and slightly confused, but she took a deep breath and tried to fake a calm expression.

"Go on…" she said.

"To my knowledge, the Snapping Turtle King is the only creature in these woods who was also alive during the days of the first Speaker. Old Cyrus must be close to one hundred summers, the poor tortured soul."

"Why tortured?" Celia asked.

"Well, he was unhinged to begin with. Any animal that trades the natural world's hierarchy for a false monarchy has lost certain mental faculties," the Lynx said.

"What do you mean?" Celia asked.

"There are no *Kings* or *Queens* in the animal world, Celia," the Lynx explained. "But poor old Cyrus was driven mad by grief long ago. All his life he has been bestowed with a very rare gift, one just as rare as you being a Speaker. But his gift has not been short-lived. He has had this gift for almost one hundred years now, and I believe it has slowly driven him mad."

"What is it?" Celia asked. The Lynx looked at her with a discerning eye, as if judging how she would receive the next piece of information.

"He is able to speak to the dead," the Lynx said plainly.

"The *dead?*" Celia gasped.

"Poor old Cyrus," the Lynx continued, "he hears the voices of animals who have died, and they, in turn, can hear him too. He can't see them, or know where they are, but he is able to call to them, and they answer."

Celia was awestruck. It seemed absolutely impossible. There was no way it could be true. But then again, it seemed inconceivable at first that she could speak to animals. And now she'd gotten very used to it.

It's possible, Celia thought, *that there are other mysteries in this universe.*

"Do you believe me?" the Lynx asked, interrupting her thoughts.

"Yes," Celia said, truthfully.

"Good. Because you must go to the Snapping Turtle King," the Lynx stated.

"Me?" Celia asked. "Why me?"

The Lynx closed his eyes so that they became nothing but two black slits in the thick fur on his face. He breathed steadily through his pink nose, emitting a low purring sound from deep within his chest.

"Celia," he said softly, "You are a Speaker for a reason. We may not understand why, it may not be our place to understand why, but there *is* a reason. I believe it may involve the Snapping Turtle King."

"I am a Speaker," Celia answered, her voice now tinged with desperation, "because I want to find my brother, wherever he is. I don't want to visit some crazy underwater reptile with a vendetta against humans. Anayla and Tippit brought me to *you* because they thought *you* could help me find my brother."

The Lynx gave a deep, labored sigh.

"Ah, yes," he said. "About your brother…"

15. The Truth

Celia stared into the Lynx's hazel eyes, not daring to break her focus. She felt her blood begin to quicken in her veins.

"What about Kyel?" she asked.

The Lynx looked back at her, and slowly everything in the cave became still. Celia was certain that there had been no movement before, but now, it was as if the stars outside had slowed, or the earth itself had stopped rotating. Her pulse, her breath, it all faded away until there was nothing. The Lynx himself appeared frozen. Then he blinked, and began to speak.

"I have the reputation of knowing the unknown," he said slowly. "And it is true that often, due to instinct or intuition, I smell truths that have not yet been spoken. But it is not through some divine knowledge; I simply watch, listen, and find the truth which is already there, but perhaps hidden from others."

"But they said you would help me find Kyel," Celia said, her voice quieting to a whisper.

"I know two things that will help you," the Lynx said. He stood and approached Celia. He brought his nose close to Celia's head and breathed in deeply, smelling her. The Lynx licked Celia's cheek with a rough, warm, sandpapery-tongue. Celia's whole body began to shake. The closeness of the animal's strength was terrifying, but there was something else building up in Celia, something that the Lynx could sense was far, far more terrifying to the young girl.

"What are the two things?" Celia asked, her jaw beginning to quiver.

"One," the Lynx said, "is that the truth is not always the first story we tell."

Celia, still sitting, placed both her hands on the ground to steady herself.

"And two," the Lynx concluded, "the last Speaker came to our woods after the death of a very, very dear loved one."

"I don't care about the other Speaker," Celia said. "I only want to know what happened to Kyel." She closed her eyes, barely controlling her own ragged breath, and repeated herself. "That is all I want to know. I only want to know what happened to Kyel and nothing else. Nothing else."

"Celia," the Lynx said, sighing heavily, "I am certain that you already know." The Lynx backed away, and lay on the floor of the cave. "Please tell me, but more importantly, tell yourself the truth."

Celia said nothing.

She opened her eyes and peered into the darkest recess of the cave. She looked at the skulls and bones stacked up in piles. She was not ready for this; not ready to think about *it* in a real sort of way. *It* was like paying bills or having a baby. *It* was something that adults dealt with, but never her. One day maybe, but not yet. But here in the cave, surrounded by the skulls and bones, *it* became natural, inevitable, equally respected and disregarded as simply what happens at a certain point of every living creature's life.

It, Celia knew, was death.

Suddenly the words, and the irrefutable facts, began to echo around the inside of Celia's skull. It started as a soft hum, and then immediately grew louder and louder until it was banging violently against the inside of her mouth, scraping on the backside of her teeth, trying to pry open her jaw and be released.

"Kyel is dead," she whispered.

The Lynx looked into her eyes. His face was calm and emotionless.

"Is that the truth?" he asked.

"That is the truth," she said. "He drowned."

"How?"

"He fell into a stream and got sucked into a drainage pipe. I didn't hear it, and I didn't see it; but that is what happened."

"How do you know?"

"The police found his body in the East River a week later," she replied.

Celia felt as if she was somewhere very, very far away, listening to her own calm voice explain the truth. This is what she had known all along. This was what she was unable to admit to herself. There was nothing left to hide now. And so she continued.

"I stood next to my parents and saw his body at the morgue before the cremation. It didn't look like him," Celia added. "It had the wrong face. It was too pale and puffy. The wrong skin color, the wrong everything, but it *was* him. I didn't want to believe that it was Kyel, so I lied to myself, I lied to my parents, and I lied to my friends. But this whole time, deep, deep down inside..." Her breath became more ragged and her shoulders began to heave up and down. Everything began to tremble.

"Be gentle with yourself, Celia," the Lynx said. He placed a paw on the ground, just in front of her.

Suddenly inside Celia, a levy was breached, and a rushing river of chaotic, frantic, frothy, murky anger, swept her away.

"I don't *want* to be gentle!" Celia yelled, standing up. "How could I be gentle? I'm furious!" She clenched her fists and screamed at the top of her lungs. "I'm so furious I could kill someone! I could rip out their heart with my bare fingernails and smash it on the floor!" Her scream echoed around the inside of the cave. It sounded like an intruder, like a trespasser in her own body.

Celia looked at the Lynx's paw reaching toward her on the ground. She kicked it as hard as she could. Then, not getting the reaction she wanted, she smashed down on it with both her fists. Despite all his power and strength, the Lynx barely reacted. He simply blinked his long eyelashes. Celia staggered backward, horrified with herself.

Then the tears that had never come before—not on the day of the terrible news, and not a single day after that—those tears, finally arrived. Large, swollen tears formed in the corners of Celia's eyes. They gathered and gathered until she felt that she was trapped underwater. She blinked and they began to pour down her face. She backed away and moved towards the cave's entrance.

"Celia," the Lynx called to her. "Go to the Snapping Turtle King," he said calmly. "I believe you can help each other."

Celia looked back at the Lynx from under her wave of confusion and horror. She could no longer speak. All the fear she felt when she first entered the cave had returned and multiplied. Any calm she had ever felt with the Lynx was now gone. Dread was everywhere. She turned and ran through the mouth of the cave and into the clear moonlight. She stumbled over a rock, but pushed herself back up. The fresh air made her feel frantic, and she continued to run through the laurel bushes and past the rock piles.

Tippit was standing right where Celia had left her with her tail wrapped carefully around her paws. She looked so tiny now, so small and helpless. The eager, expectant look in Tippit's eyes crushed Celia. She knew she had given her friend false hopes about finding Kyel, and seeing it there in Tippit's eyes just made Celia's own pain expand.

"What did you find out?" Tippit called. Celia ran until she was standing directly in front of Tippit, gasping and choking from the tears of anger streaming down her face.

"Get away from me!" Celia screamed. Tippit's eyes grew wide with confusion. "You are the worst friend EVER!" Celia yelled. "I knew it was a terrible idea to go into the cave! I didn't want to go in there!"

"Wh-what happened?" Tippit stammered. "I...I don't understand."

"You have done nothing to help me, NOTHING!" Celia yelled. "Leave me alone, and don't try to find me! I don't *ever* want to see you again!"

Before Tippit could ask anything else, Celia was running as fast as she could down the hill. She crashed blindly through the woods, falling and then getting up and still running, her tears and mucus choking her. Her lungs were burning. They were heaving and suffocating as she ran. They felt the way they did the night her Gran left to return to Jamaica. Or when her mother put all of Kyel's belongings into boxes.

No, the burning was worse than that.

Her lungs felt like the day her father brought home a small capsule, an urn, with Kyel's cremated ashes in it and asked Celia where she wanted to spread them. She yelled at him. She *screamed* at him that she didn't care, because it wasn't Kyel in there. Then she had run to her bedroom, to her and Kyel's bedroom, and pulled their mobile from the ceiling and trampled it to pieces. Then, for reasons she still didn't understand, she shoved all the pieces into a trash bag and shoved them down her building's garbage chute. She remembered how her parents stood in the bedroom doorway and watched her, terrified, crying big silent tears, but all the while, allowed her to do what she was doing. At that moment she had thought to herself, *Kyel can't be dead, because I haven't cried.* Somehow the twisted logic had made sense at that time. And it had stuck.

Now the tears were here. And it was as if they were gathering in a tar pit for her to run through. Everything that Celia had tried so carefully not to feel, was now reaching up and pulling her down. There was the despair for losing Kyel; the guilt for being at the stream when he was whisked away and not even hearing it; the terror of Kyel's bloated, deformed corpse at the morgue; the anger at the world for continuing after Kyel's death; the shame for lying to Violet and Susan; and the guilt of tricking Tippit and Anayla into thinking Kyel could still be found. But above all this was the the shock that one day her Gran, her parents, everyone she ever knew or loved, even she herself, would die.

Every emotion reached up and grabbed her body, pulling her to the ground or thrashing her into trees, making her stumble and stagger like she was fighting invisible demons.

Celia didn't know where she was going, but she kept moving downhill the whole way. When the ground leveled off, she ran in the direction of the moon. When she was certain that she was lost and would never find camp or a road or a house again, she practically ran straight into a building.

It was the bike shed. She clutched the side of the small structure crying and gasping for breath. She threw up a little bit. When she caught her breath enough to focus her vision, she turned around and looked behind her.

Tippit was not there.

Good, she thought, which made her cry a little harder.

Celia staggered down the moonlit paths towards the middle of camp. When she made it to the center of the Nesting Grove, she collapsed.

16. The Cupcake

It was just before sunrise as Susan headed toward the Chow Lodge once again to battle with the faulty oven, which was quickly becoming her archnemesis. She was armed with a wrench, her trusty clipboard, and pure determination that *this* time she would fix the darn thing for good, when suddenly she stumbled over something. Large.

It was Celia.

Crumpled in the grass.

Susan let out a yelp of shock, at first assuming the worst. Then she saw Celia's shoulders rise and fall with breath. Susan steadied her trembling hands, and gently shook Celia awake.

"Celia?" she whispered.

"Leave me alone…" Celia responded groggily. The skin around her eyes looked swollen. Her lips were dried and cracked, exposing softer, pink skin that must have stung in the chilled morning air.

"Celia!" Susan repeated.

"Left alone…" Celia murmured.

Susan carefully tucked the wrench and clipboard into her shorts waistband and used both arms to lug and prop Celia up onto her feet. Then, step by step, she carefully led Celia, one foot in front of the other, back across the Great Lawn towards the Cupcake.

Mrs. Nalgy awoke to the sound of desperate banging on the door.

"Tetanus!" she yelled out with a start. Then she quickly came to her senses and opened the door in her night robe and curlers. There before her was Susan barely holding up the long arms and legs of an unconscious—or uncooperative—she couldn't tell which, camper.

"Oh, my Doc Susie Anderson!" Mrs. Nalgy whispered to herself. Then she sprang to action. Together the two women dragged Celia into the Cupcake and over to one of the cots. They took off Celia's wet shoes and clothes and changed her into a dry sweatshirt and sweatpants and tucked a warm blanket around her. Celia felt a thermometer poke into her mouth and find its place under her tongue. She clamped down on the metallic-tasting tip. Just as a kettle began to boil, the thermometer was pulled out of her mouth.

"Mmmmmm hmm," she heard Mrs. Nalgy inspect the thermometer. Then there was a slight scuffle on the floorboards, and Celia opened her eyes as Susan tried to hand her a warm mug of peppermint tea. She closed her eyes again and began to slump to one side. Mrs. Nalgy swiftly grabbed Celia's shoulders and propped her upright with the help of three firm pillows.

Mrs. Nalgy then tried to give Celia a bowl of something warm and steaming. Celia could smell oatmeal, brown sugar, and melted butter wafting from the bowl. Perhaps there was even a little clover honey in the mix. Without a word, Celia turned her head away and squeezed her swollen eyes tighter.

Then Mrs. Nalgy spoke. Her words were kind, but *very* firm.

"Open up those beautiful eyes, Celia," she said. "You need to eat."

Celia opened her stinging eyes halfway and took the bowl from Mrs. Nalgy. The first gulp sent warmth oozing all through her body. Celia also took the mug and drank the tea slowly, with eyes half-opened. The pepperminty tingle warmed her throat and chest, and made her head feel a little clearer.

Mrs. Nalgy waved Susan over to the other side of the Cupcake to stand by the tiny stove and talk in a hushed tone. Celia strained to hear them.

"Is she alright?" Susan whispered.

"She looks fine to me," Mrs. Nalgy said. "Normal temperature. Just over-tired, and possibly a bit dehydrated."

"I found her asleep in the middle of the Nesting Grove."

"Well, that would explain part of it," Mrs. Nalgy said, not in the least bit shaken or surprised. It made Celia wonder what else Mrs. Nalgy has encountered over her thirty years as Camp Nurse.

Susan made her voice even softer. "This is Celia Johnson. The camper whose father called on Monday."

"Oh, yes," Mrs. Nalgy replied, understanding.

"Do you think I should I call her parents?" Susan asked.

"NO!" Celia yelled. The spoon jangled loudly against the side of the ceramic bowl as she jolted straight up on the cot. Susan looked at her with surprise, Mrs. Nalgy with a raised eyebrow. Celia slumped back down into the pillows and quietly finished devouring the oatmeal.

Mrs. Nalgy, turned back to Susan with a hushed voice. "I don't think it's necessary to worry them," she said. "This child just needs some rest and fluids."

Susan looked at Mrs. Nalgy, and then at Celia whose eyes were closed again.

"Are you sure she's alright?" Susan whispered. Celia couldn't help but feel flattered by the honest concern in Susan's voice.

"I'm very certain, my dear, that she will be fine," Mrs. Nalgy replied. "You go help Aggie and Ma with the stoves. Leave Celia with me. Some rest will have her back on her feet in no time," she vowed as she ushered Susan back out the door.

Celia heard the door click behind Susan. Then she heard Mrs. Nalgy's slippers shuffling back into the room. She didn't feel like talking or answering any questions, so she quickly closed her eyes and pretended to sleep. Mrs. Nalgy took the emptied bowl from Celia's hands. She felt Celia's forehead for a few seconds, and apparently satisfied with whatever she found, shuffled away.

After a few minutes of Mrs. Nalgy's slippers scuffling around the Cupcake, Celia heard the creak of her rotund body settling back into her own rickety cot. Then there were no sounds at all besides a few songbirds beginning to welcome the dawn. Celia could understand the words to the chorus as more and more birds joined in to sing together. The song was something about sunlight springing fresh onto the first dewfall. Celia put the pillow over her ears to smother away the noise of the sweet, hopeful song. She shifted her body so that she faced the white wall. She focused on nothing, absolutely nothing.

Kyel is dead.

The thought just popped right into her head. She closed her eyes, and repeated it over and over and over in her mind…

Kyel is dead.

Kyel is dead.

Kyel is dead.

… until she felt burning tears slipping through her scrunched eyelids. She cried silently until she fell asleep.

17. The Remainder of That Day

Celia slept for the remainder of that day. She woke briefly in the early evening to slurp down a bowl of tortilla soup that Aggie had carried over from the Chow Hall. Then she fell back asleep and didn't wake up for the rest of that night.

18. That Night

That night Celia tossed and turned from the worst nightmares since Kyel's death. They were the same dreams about Kyel at the edge of a tall building, or climbing a cracking tree branch, or balancing on separating and shifting scaffolding – but this time Kyel was not Kyel. He *looked* like Kyel from the back, but when Celia screamed to him, he actually turned around. But instead of Kyel's face, there was a horrible, pale, bloated face with no eyes, and a wide, gaping mouth that just opened and closed like it was trying to breathe, or maybe say something, but couldn't.

Mrs. Nalgy woke that night to the sounds of Celia crying in her sleep. She put a cold washcloth over the sleeping girl's forehead, but didn't wake her. Mrs. Nalgy knew Celia needed to wrestle with her nightmares on her own. Waking her would only prolong the process. Mrs. Nalgy shuttered remembering the nightmares she herself had suffered after Mr. Nalgy passed away. With a tear in her eye, she patted the washcloth gently against Celia's sweating forehead, and repeated a silent prayer of support.

Lord, help this child to find her way through the dreaded wilderness of grief. Help her to remain strong and reclaim the peace in her heart.

19. Edith's Journal

The following morning Celia woke to a light tapping on the door. She had no memory of her dreams from the night before, just a cold, tired feeling in her bones.

"Is Celia here?" Violet's voice asked.

"She is, my dear, but she's sleeping," Mrs. Nalgy replied.

"Is she ok?" Violet asked.

"She's fine dear, just resting."

"Can I wake her up to say hi?" Violet's voice sounded hopeful but realistically doubtful at the same time.

"This isn't a good time, dear," Mrs. Nalgy said. Celia heard the door shut, and Violet walking away. *Not sprinting,* Celia thought, *just walking.*

The next time Celia opened her eyes, Violet's prism was resting on a small table beside her cot. Without touching the prism, Celia turned onto her other shoulder so that she faced the white wall.

Kyel is dead, she thought.

No tears this time. Just a numb, exhausted feeling behind her eyes and a hollow feeling in her chest.

She closed her eyes and fell asleep again. Her nightmares were waiting for her the moment she drifted off. But this time, she did not call out to the horrible, pale, bloated, eyeless monster. Instead, Celia watched him fall off the building, clutching the broken railing;

she watched him crash down the length of the tree still clutching the broken branch; she watched the scaffolding slip and collapse in a large dusty pile with him buried somewhere deep inside. But she did not scream. Somehow she knew, as she watched all these horrors unfold before her eyes, that it was not really Kyel. He was already gone.

Hours later, Celia awoke to another knock on the door. She kept her eyes tightly closed as she listened to Mrs. Nalgy shuffle across the Cupcake to see who was there.

"Oh, Susan," she said. "Come on in." And then after a moment she asked, "How'd it go with the stove?"

"Wrong part," Susan sighed.

"Ahhh," Mrs. Nalgy replied without much concern.

"Is she asleep?" Susan asked. The voices were pointed in Celia's direction now.

"I'm not sure," Mrs. Nalgy said. "But her eyes are closed at any rate."

"I brought her this," Susan said.

"Oh!" Mrs. Nalgy said. Her voice momentarily caught in her throat. She cleared it. "How very clever and thoughtful of you, my dear," she said, muffled this time as if the two women were hugging.

There was a bit more shuffling. Then Celia heard Susan's footsteps approach the cot.

"This is for you to borrow," Susan whispered. "I've read it many times, but I don't really understand it. I think it might make more sense to you... and I hope it helps."

Susan placed something on the table and left the Cupcake.

Celia waited until Mrs. Nalgy had to leave on a nursing call before she opened her eyes. It was mid-afternoon, and the room was bathed in peaceful silence. Sunlight streamed in against the white walls.

On the small table, beside Violet's prism, sat a plain, brown notebook. Celia studied it for a moment. She could see that it was very old and worn, but clean of any dust. It was the size of a regular composition notebook, like the kind she used in school, with a strip of cloth for the binding. The only difference between this notebook, and the black and white speckled one she had for school, was that this one was plain brown all over.

Celia reached for the book and opened the front cover. The spine was supple as if it had been opened thousands of times before. She flipped through the thin, lined pages. They were bumpy and covered with handwritten words. The penmanship was clear, crisp script, easy to read. Celia flipped back to the inside cover.

It said, *"Edith Glynwood – 1935."*

Susan's grandmother's journal. Celia flipped to the first page and immediately began reading.

May 24, 1935

"I feel completely alone in this world. Mother died fifteen years ago, and now father died two nights ago in his sleep. I found him in the morning. I buried him. And now I have nothing. What good is this cabin or the land to me now? Without family? A day's ride away from the closest neighbor? I cannot rest, or eat. I just cry and retch. I will probably die of sorrow and fear before the first chill of autumn arrives to the woods."

Celia continued, flipping quickly through the pages, reading the words that described each day and week of loneliness as it passed. Then she slowed, almost to a stop, at a particular entry.

June 29, 1935

"*Death was hovering above the cabin, waiting to take me with him. At least he was before the very strange events of today. I have met a friend. A very unlikely friend. I met her in the woods. I cannot explain who, or how… because I would think I am going crazy even to see the words written in my own handwriting. But still I am sure of what happened. I will simply refer to her as "my friend." At first I was afraid of her. But then, the fear passed, and was replaced by curiosity. She is very kind. I have a new feeling of hope after today. I will see my friend again tomorrow. We will meet on the mountain ridge, above the cabin.*"

Celia read this entry a second time.

Then a third.

Could it be? she wondered. She continued reading, careful not to rip the pages as she turned them, devouring the words hungrily.

Hours later as daylight faded, Celia looked up from the journal to the sound of the Cupcake door slamming shut. Mrs. Nalgy stood in the center of the room, observing Celia awake and reading. Celia flinched, worried that now she would finally have to explain what she was doing out of her dorm past Lights Out. But Mrs. Nalgy moved across the room without a word. She rummaged through a cabinet by the stove, and produced a flashlight. Then, without a single word, she placed the flashlight on the small table by Celia's cot, and prepared herself for bed. When Mrs. Nalgy shut off the light to go to sleep, Celia clicked on the flashlight and continued reading.

In the deepest depth of night, Celia finished reading the last page of the journal and clicked off the flashlight. She sat silently on the cot in the darkness, rubbing her tired eyes. The voice of the young woman, Edith Glynwood, still rang in her ears. Her mind spun wildly, trying to make sense of everything. She felt certain from what she read that Edith had been the first Speaker, and that the "friend" described in these pages was the Lynx's mother.

But the entries ended at the last page of the notebook, in the middle of the summer, and didn't tell her everything she needed to know. They said nothing about a Snapping Turtle, or Edith losing her power of being a Speaker. Maybe Celia had missed something. She clicked the flashlight on again and flipped back to the first page. She began reading again, this time slowly and with more concentration.

"I feel completely alone in this world," the first line read.

20. Rearranging Letters

The next morning Celia woke up slumped against the wall, still hunched over Edith's journal. She had fallen asleep reading some time just before dawn. She closed the notebook and slipped it under her pillow. Then she rotated her crimped neck and stretched her legs so that the cot creaked.

For the first time, she felt the warmth and comfort of the soft cotton Camp Glynwood sweatshirt and sweatpants, and the springy lightness of the mattress beneath her. She lay down and allowed herself to doze gently in and out of a peaceful sleep. When she awoke the next time, there was a warm mug of peppermint tea waiting on the table. She took a sip and settled back onto the pillow. Her head felt light, almost pleasant. She drifted back to sleep.

The next time she opened her eyes, there was a covered plate of scrambled eggs with hot sauce from Aggie. Celia's jean shorts, white t-shirt, and Dodgers sweatshirt had also appeared at the foot of her bed, folded and freshly laundered. Celia found that there was a patch of matching black material stitched over the tear in the sweatshirt's sleeve. She traced the hand-stitched needlework with one of her fingers, and looked over at Mrs. Nalgy who was counting boxes of Band-Aids.

"Did you patch my sleeve?" Celia asked Mrs. Nalgy.

"Sure," came the reply.

"Thank you," Celia said. Mrs. Nalgy nodded and chortled to herself.

"It was certainly less squirmy and much quieter than giving a child stitches, I'll tell you that."

Celia winced at the thought, then slipped the clothes on under the blankets, happy to be back in her regular life uniform.

Realizing that Mrs. Nalgy had no intention of grilling her with questions, Celia quit pretending to sleep for the rest of the day. She watched Mrs. Nalgy putter around the small, oddly shaped cabin, taking care of the things that needed taking care of. She also reread the journal for the third time. This time she skipped around to the passages she found the most interesting.

Early in the afternoon, just after the Time Gong sounded off two times, there was a loud knock at the door.

"Is Celia still here?" Violet's voice asked.

"She is, my dear," Mrs. Nalgy replied, shooting a glance over at Celia who was sitting up, reading.

"Can I come in and visit her?" Violet blurted out, "I wanted to tell her I got into Sculpture Shop this rotation."

"No, dear," Mrs. Nalgy said, looking over at Celia, "she's fast asleep."

Mrs. Nalgy quickly shooed Violet away. Celia set down the journal, losing her place in the process.

"Why did you say that?" she asked, surprised. Mrs. Nalgy shot her a sly look, then busied herself again with arranging some medication bottles on the shelf.

"If you want the *company* of the living, my dear, then you have to *join* the living," she said.

Celia watched Mrs. Nalgy for a few seconds. Then she flipped back through the pages of the journal to find her place.

"How are you finding your reading?" Mrs. Nalgy asked absentmindedly.

"Very interesting," Celia answered, looking at her. Neither of them said anything for a few minutes. Then Celia decided to test the waters.

"Why do you think Susan let me borrow this?" she asked.

"Well," said Mrs. Nalgy, "I suppose that's the year Edith's – that's Mrs. Glynwood to you – it was the year her father died. It was a very, very dark time for her. And perhaps Susan thought it might help you to read about someone else who..." Mrs. Nalgy's voice trailed off.

"Had lost someone they loved a lot," Celia finished her sentence.

Mrs. Nalgy nodded and smiled sadly.

"Do you know if there are other journals?" Celia asked.

"Oh, sure. Susan found a whole series of them, almost fifty years' worth, when old Edith passed away. Turns out she was quite the avid writer. Not that any of us ever saw her sit still long enough to touch pen to paper. But there were probably other things we didn't know about her, too. She was a private person really, although most people never realized it since she surrounded herself with so much life."

"Did you know Mrs. Glynwood well?" Celia asked.

"Yes, dear. She was like a mother to me." Mrs. Nalgy smiled. "But, she was like that for many girls."

"Where are the other journals?" Celia asked. "I would really like to read the one that comes right after this one."

"I don't know. I suppose they're probably all locked away in the Chow Lodge's attic. The Chow Lodge used to be the Glynwood family cabin, before Edith converted the land to a girls' camp."

"Oh," said Celia, quietly.

"But if you want to read more," Mrs. Nalgy continued, "you'll have to talk to Susan, and *that*, my dear," she hoisted a thumb toward the door for emphasis, "also requires *joining* the living." She winked and turned her back to Celia and began shuffling papers around inside a filing cabinet.

Just then a younger, timid Glynwood Girl came in leading another girl by the hand. The second girl was crying loudly as blood poured from her knee. Mrs. Nalgy talked to them both in a soothing voice as she unlocked the newly installed padlock on the medicine cabinet and doused the cut with Rubbing Alcohol.

"Nothing to worry about, my dears," she said. "We'll just clean this cut out and you'll be as good as new."

Before the girls left, Mrs. Nalgy gave each of them a handshake for their bravery. Then she placed the medicine cabinet's key on a hook hidden behind the clock hanging over the stovetop, and went to her desk to fill out some paperwork.

Celia sighed and turned her attention back to the journal. She read one particular passage over again.

"Somehow, I was lost. Lost without ever leaving where I had always been. My world was not the same. But slowly, thankfully, I know where I am again. The world is different now. New and not yet familiar, but I can see that one day, it could be just as wonderful. Maybe even more wonderful than before."

Celia thought about an unhappy Edith, imagining a happier future. She listened to the sounds drifting through the air around her. There was the rhythmic pulse of drumming, the zipping of a zip-line from the ropes course, splashing and shrieking from the Lake, and the distant bouncing of a basketball. She heard the strumming of a guitar meandering through the trees and a group of girls singing. It was a slow song, sort of sad, but Celia thought that it sounded pretty the way the voices were learning to harmonize. They made her think of the sweet and hopeful birds in the morning.

When the first song was over, the girls began singing a new one that was fast, with tongue-twisting words that told a silly tale about the ingredients for a crazy soup. She could make out mothballs, cannonballs, lima beans, gasoline, among the many other unlikely rhyming ingredients, before the song ended in a flurry of guitar strumming and laughter. Without realizing it, there was a subtle shift in Celia's heart, similar to the one the journal was trying to describe. She wanted to know all the words to that song. She wanted to sit with the other girls and sing the chorus faster and faster until they all burst out laughing together.

Later that afternoon Mrs. Nalgy left the Cupcake to inspect a possibly fractured ankle on the tennis courts. The room was empty and silent. Celia's attention drifted away from the journal to watch a beam of sunlight shift across the white walls until it rested on the prism. Tiny rainbows bounced all over the Cupcake. Celia stared at them trying to focus mostly on the blank space beside violet where ultraviolet would be; that powerful force that existed just beyond the visible spectrum, as Violet had put it.

Kyel is dead, she thought. The fact just popped back into her mind.

But it was different now. She felt quiet inside.

She picked up the prism and tried to remember her life before Kyel. Her life before she felt so lost. She thought about her mother reading *Alice's Adventures in Wonderland* to her when she was little. She closed her eyes and was curled with her mother on their couch. Celia was four-years-old again and practically intoxicated by the warmth of her mother's skin and the excitement in her voice. Her mother was pregnant with Kyel, but he wasn't a part of their life yet, and yet they were happy.

Celia's mom read from the adult version of *Alice's Adventures in Wonderland*. It was a copy of Lewis Carroll's book that she had kept from her college days when she was still in Jamaica studying to become an English teacher. Celia gently brushed the annotated and dog-eared pages with her tiny fingers as if shining a sacred jewel. The book was hundreds of pages long, filled with grown-up language. Four-year-old Celia didn't understand some parts of it, but it never bothered her. She cherished that time she had with her mother, nestled closely against her mother's side, wrapped together in a cocoon of warmth and imagination. Every time Celia's mom finished reading for the night, she closed the cover, and Celia would beg her to show her how to rearrange the golden embossed letters A-L-I-C-E from the title into C-E-L-I-A. Then her mother would explain why she had named her Celia, instead of Alice.

Celia blinked tears away. She missed her mother. And her father. And come to think of it, she missed Violet, too. She missed the "company of the living," as Mrs. Nalgy had put it. She missed them almost as much as she missed Kyel, except there was something she could actually do about it. Celia tied the prism's leather cord tightly around her wrist.

Tomorrow morning, Celia would *"join the living."* She would go to breakfast and sit with her Dorm Sisters. She would learn the words to that silly soup song and maybe meet some of the other girls she hadn't yet had the chance to meet. Then she would find Violet and tell her what she's known all along but had just been holding back, about Kyel, and the reasons behind her name.

But first, there was something else she needed to do.

The Lynx had been right: being a Speaker was never about finding Kyel. Despite keeping the truth buried deep under her sadness, she had known about his death all along. There must be another reason why she had been given this amazing gift. As long as she still had the power to speak with the animals, there was still more for her to learn.

Tonight, she would go back into the woods.

First, she would find Tippit and apologize.

Then, she would go to the Snapping Turtle King.

21. The Stone Forest

That night in the Cupcake, Celia waited to hear Mrs. Nalgy's soft snoring before she slipped out the screen door. Her body felt rested and strong as she jogged down the dark path to the Nesting Grove. The moon had just reached the tip of the pine tree at the center of the dorms when Celia slipped into the woods and found the clearing where she and Tippit usually met. The clearing was empty, so Celia chose a small rock and sat down to wait. The woods were stark and motionless under the moonlight, like a black and white photograph taken of trees and grass that had turned to stone.

Celia waited for over two hours. When the moon was halfway down the pine tree, she knew Tippit wasn't coming. Celia thought about her last words to Tippit, shouted in desperation and rage. She pictured her friend's golden eyes stretched wide with confusion and fear. Knowing she couldn't find the fox's den on her own, Celia's heart felt as still and cold as the stone forest around her.

Celia walked back to the Nesting Grove. She paused to stand among the sleeping dorms. It occurred to her that she had seen more of this camp in moonlight than she had in sunlight. She raised her eyes to the pale crescent moon. It looked lonely and cold. Celia suddenly imagined standing on the moon, alone and hundreds of thousands of miles away from any other living organism. She remembered what Violet had said about Jupiter, with its sixty-two confirmed moons. She thought about sixty-two moons, each lonelier and colder than the next, orbiting around the same giant planet, but never, ever sitting down to a meal, or laughing, or singing together. She considered herself, her parents and their silent apartment after Kyel had died. *We were moons*, she thought, *orbiting our grief.*

A shiver shook Celia and she noticed that she was standing next to Great Dorm 8; Violet's dorm. Between her and the dorm was a wooden post with a clipboard nailed to it. A pencil dangled from an Activities Sign-Up sheet. Celia stared at it. Then, she took the pencil in her hand and scribbled out a note on a piece of paper from the clipboard. It said:

> *Dear Violet,*
> *My brother Kyel drowned in April.*
> *That isn't what I think.*
> *It's what really happened.*
> > *Your friend,*
> > *Celia*

Celia rolled the paper into a tight, little scroll and stuck it through a hole in the screened window near Violet's bed. After leaving the note, the ground under her red Keds felt a little warmer and more alive. There were earthworms beneath her feet, she was sure, and fireflies above her head, and little critters in the trees. There were ferns growing on the sides of the path, and moss slowly covering rocks. She existed on a living, breathing planet, she told herself, filled with hundreds of thousands of living, breathing organisms. Not a moon.

Unsure of what else to do, Celia slipped back toward the

Cupcake. Just as she was carefully opening the screen door, she heard a low, grumbling voice muttering to itself. Thinking that Mrs. Nalgy was awake, Celia froze. But Mrs. Nalgy, was in fact, still tucked comfortably in her cot, fast asleep with a thin string of drool delicately dangling from her mouth. Celia scanned the Cupcake's interior and watched with utter disbelief as a small patch of the wooden floor lifted into the air and hovered like a U.F.O.

"Hello?" Celia whispered. Instantly, the small patch of floor clattered back into place. She heard scuffling under the floorboards, and watched something furry shake the bushes just behind the Cupcake. Without hesitation, Celia quietly closed the door, and sprang down the steps. She ran through the bushes where they were still swishing from side to side.

"Tippit?" she whispered. No answer. She followed the sway of the undergrowth just a few steps further. Still finding nothing, she continued on.

When she was far enough into the woods that no one back at camp could hear, she yelled, "TIPPIT! I'm sorry!"

Something shook the bushes just ahead of her. There was more grumbling. Celia ran in a full sprint toward the noise.

22. Otto and Keen

Celia heard the small river before she saw it. Although she tried to slow her forward movement, she still burst through the bushes and was suddenly balancing on the slippery edge of rushing water. She frantically waved her arms backward to keep from toppling in. For three rapid breaths she panicked, but then she looked closer and saw it was just a tiny river. Practically a small stream. Only a trickle in some places. Still, she couldn't help but think about the stream behind her school, the one that whisked Kyel away.

Celia was staring into the river's tiny eddies and swirling whirlpools, when something shifted in the bushes a few feet away from her. As she turned, she heard a different rushing noise. It was the rush of air passing through outstretched wings. A deafening screech pierced the night from above. The leaves on the ground around her feet quickly scattered. Confused and distracted, Celia was still looking down when the first sharp blow struck her on the back of the head. Celia whirled around. There was nothing there. She touched her head where the pain was blossoming.

Blood trickled down her fingers.

The deafening screech sounded out again. A rush of air grazed her left shoulder, just barely missing her ear. When the maddening cry rang out a third time, Celia dropped to the ground and pulled her head toward her chest. She grabbed a large fallen branch and waved it wildly above her body at whatever was attacking her. She turned just in time to see a feathery blur shoot past her face. This time she made out a yellow, knife-like beak snapping in protest as the streak of brown feathers was further enraged at having something heaved at it. Already it was gone again, swooping a wide arc in the night sky. It hovered for a moment, turned, and then dive-bombed again, this time aiming directly for Celia's head.

Suddenly, there was a loud splashing commotion from the riverbank beside her.

"FOR THE LOVE OF ALL THINGS SCALED AND SLIMEY, BACK DOWN, BIRD! BACK DOWN!" boomed a thunderous voice.

A large, brown otter emerged, hobbling from the river right beside Celia's head. Her attacker came to an immediate halt mid-dive, and gracefully floated down to the grass beside the otter's feet.

To Celia's surprise those sharp talons and beak belonged to a bird no larger than a robin. Her vicious assailant was only a tiny, ruffled-feathered Saw-whet owl that was breathing so heavily with excitement that his little heart practically pounded through his chest.

"Did I do good? Did I do good, Otto? Did I? Huh? Huh? Huh?" The bird twittered quickly as his gigantic, round eyes darted from Celia, to the large otter standing next to her, and back again, and back again.

As Celia caught her breath, still curled on the ground clutching the tree branch, she became aware of a rancid smell wafting from the otter's direction. Never blinking, the tiny owl stared at the stinky otter, waiting for a reply.

But the otter did not reply. He was too busy flicking twigs and bits of reeds off his slick, brown fur. Celia pushed the tree branch aside and sat up to get a better look at the otter. She had seen them in books and on TV, but never in real life. He was about the size of a very large cat, but he walked on his hind legs.

"For the love of the forest and all things green..." the otter muttered under his breath. "Leave the human alone and let's be on our way." But his breath! The stench reached Celia's nostrils again. It was a dank, fishy smell, like the murkiest bog, and something else sharp that she could not quite name.

"Did I do good?" the Saw-whet owl asked again, still without blinking his large, perfectly round, yellow eyes.

The otter ignored the bird and instead, to Celia's shock, focused on using his nimble paws to unscrew the cap of a bottle with clear liquid inside. The otter's clawed fingers held the bottle crookedly, and his mouth covered most of the opening, as he gulped down the remaining contents. It was one of the missing bottles of Rubbing Alcohol from the Cupcake.

Celia stared at the otter holding the glass bottle. Once she had seen a farmer feed a young calf from a baby's bottle on a field trip to Long Island. She had also seen crows delicately eat corn on the cob from a dumpster behind a restaurant. And once in a city park, she had even seen a raccoon use its tiny paws to open a trashcan and pick pieces of meat, but no onions, out of a Chinese food carton. But she had never, ever, seen an animal drink from a bottle on its own.

The otter let out a massive burp.

The rush of putrid air was so foul it made Celia dry heave. It even made the small owl's constant barrage of questions momentarily stop.

Then it continued.

"Did you even see, Otto? Did you see? How was it? Did I do good? Did I?" The otter still ignored the owl.

"You did very *well*, silly bird," Celia finally replied. "You got me twice right on the back of my head."

The owl and otter froze. They turned slowly and looked at her. The otter's mouth hung open. From it wafted the revolting smell. His bristly whiskers twitched with curiosity as he studied her carefully through long eyelashes.

"KEEN!" the otter yelled to the owl. Both Keen and Celia jumped.

"KEEN!" the otter repeated, "I BELIEVE WE HAVE FOUND..." the otter shook his head to the left, then to the right. A small gush of water poured out of his ears.

"I believe we have found," he said now talking at regular volume, "a speaking human."

"The other animals call me a Speaker," Celia confirmed. Both animals continued staring at her. Then the otter burped again.

Celia quickly pinched her nose to protect herself from the smell. Keen momentarily closed his eyes and leaned to the left, as if about to faint. Then he opened his eyes, snapped to attention, and straightened up.

"Oh, we've been hearing about you," Keen said, fluffing his feathers with his sharp little beak. "Word travels fast around the woods," he added.

"Did you come alone, Speaker?" Otto asked, sniffing the air.

"Yes," Celia said.

"So you're a Speaker *and* a liar," Otto mumbled, "Charming combination."

"No, really," Celia insisted, "I'm here by myself."

Otto stared at her, studying her face for a moment.

"Well, add stupidity to the mix then," he said dismissively.

Celia took a deep breath and swallowed hard to keep down her bubbling frustration.

"My name is Celia," she said, as friendly as she could. Otto rolled his eyes.

"I'm Otto," the otter said matter-of-factly, "and this is Keen," he pointed to the owl. "We don't care about you, and you don't care about us. Mice meat to you and goodbye, lying, human Speaker child." Otto dropped down onto all four feet and began slinking through the reeds toward the river.

Celia shook off the lying comment and smiled to herself, thinking of the kits. Word sure does travel fast in the woods, she thought. Then she realized that Otto and Keen had almost disappeared into the dark undergrowth.

"Wait!" she yelled. "Do you know a fox named Tippit?"

"Fox?!" Otto yelled over his shoulder. "I don't associate with foxes. They can't be trusted."

"Not this fox," Celia insisted. "She's caring and kind and she tried to help me."

"Doesn't matter," Otto said.

"Wait! Please!" she begged. "I need to find her. I need to thank her...and apologize..."

"Disperse, Keen. Disperse," Otto said over his back. "We have nothing to say to this human child that speaks and lies."

Accepting orders, Keen flew into the trees and perched on a branch. He turned his back to Celia and tucked his head under one wing, practically disappearing as he became nothing more than a tiny, brown lump on the tree branch. A feeling of panic washed over Celia.

Then she spotted the small clear bottle left on the ground next to the river. She scooped it up and tipped it towards her nose. There were a few drops of liquid still left.

"You may not care about me," she yelled, holding up the bottle, "but you care about this!"

Otto turned and eyed the contents in Celia's hands.

Suddenly, the otter was transformed into a sputtering, hissing, cursing mess, moving quickly toward Celia, swiping the air around him with sharp claws and gnashing his little, terribly sharp teeth.

"GIVE THAT TO ME!" he thundered. "KEEN! ATTACK! ATTACK! GET THAT BOTTLE OR I WILL SEND YOUR CARCASS TO THE MOON!"

Before Keen could even leave his perch, Celia threw the bottle at Otto's feet. The snarling animal lunged and swiped the bottle up, guzzling down the last few drops.

Keen floated down from the tree and landed softly on the ground next to Celia. He eyed his friend nervously. In the silence that followed, Otto threw down the bottle, gasped deeply, wiped his mouth, and then slowly looked up at Keen.

23. The Deal

"Sorry, little fellow," Otto said softly, his harsh words still echoing in the silent woods. "I lost myself for a moment there."

Otto's beautiful hazel eyes opened wide as he looked to see if his friend would accept the apology. Keen began ruffling his feathers with his beak, grooming his side, and busily looking away.

Otto stood up and took in a deep breath. His belly and chest grew.

"Come here, Keen," Otto said gruffly. The little bird flapped his wings but stayed where he was. Otto righted the bottle carefully on the ground, then limped slowly to Keen and began petting the bird softly on his head.

"Fine job, Keen," he said quietly. "A fine job as always, my friend. I'm sorry for that." Keen nodded his feathery head, and without another word, the rift between them was over.

Celia cleared her throat to remind them she was still there.

"What do you want?" Otto asked, glancing at her.

"I need to find the fox named Tippit," she said. "She was helping me look for my brother... but the truth is, we were never going to find him because ...well, he died. But I wanted to thank Tippit, all the same, for being a good friend and trying to help."

Otto looked at her carefully. Then he looked away to somewhere downstream. Something in his gaze told Celia he was looking to a place far beyond where she could see, to a real place that Otto had once known well.

"I'm sorry for your loss," he said quietly still petting Keen's head, "but we all have our own losses, and I keep out of human business as a strict policy."

Keen's eyes were now closed and he cooed softly, as if entranced.

Otto's words echoed softly in Celia's mind. *We all have our own losses...*

Celia thought about Tippit's sister, and how she never even asked about her. She also thought about Violet, Susan, Edith, and even Mrs. Nagly – each with their own loss.

"I also need to get to the Snapping Turtle King," Celia said, suddenly remembering and breaking the silence.

Otto's hand froze, hovering in mid-air, no longer petting Keen.

Keen's eyes opened.

They both looked at Celia. And blinked.

"*What?*" Otto whispered in a bellow of disbelief. "You have no business going to the..." Otto hushed his voice and shook his head. "That's the *last* place a human Speaker should go."

"I need to see him," Celia said.

"Don't you know the story?" Keen asked, his little tufted head rotating on his neck to get a better look at Celia. "The last Speaker killed the Queen."

"Yes," Celia said, lifting her chin trying to look brave. "I've heard the story."

Otto shook his head. "Absolutely not," he said. "We'll have no part in it. We stay out of human business, Speaker or not. That's our strict policy." He turned again and began walking away.

Celia thought about Tippit. She thought about the fox's face the last time she'd seen it, crushed by her anger. Then she thought about Kyel. Both of them seemed to be fading further and further away with every step Otto took. Her options swirled above her like a mobile tipped off balance and spinning wildly.

"Wait!" Celia yelled with desperation. She picked up the bottle. "Where did this come from, then? This is from the human world. This is human business that you don't mind getting involved with."

Otto and Keen both looked at Celia.

Then at the bottle.

Then at Celia. Then at the bottle, again.

They both blinked.

"If you help me find the fox," Celia said slowly, "and bring me to the Snapping Turtle King, I will bring you more bottles." Celia could see Otto's mind weighing his options. There was a silent battle taking place behind his eyes. Celia advanced her approach.

"The cabinet is locked now," she said slowly, "you saw it for yourself. But I know where the key is. If you find the fox, and promise to show me the way to the Snapping Turtle King, I will meet you tomorrow with as many bottles as you want."

Otto just stared at her.

"Go away, human child," Keen said quietly in a fearful twitter, taking a fluttering hop backwards. "Don't do this..." he pleaded.

Otto's whiskers began to twitch with curiosity.

Celia continued, looking only at Otto.

"Plus," she went on, "I have hands with fingers, and opposable thumbs, and long arms. Do you know how many of those bottles I could carry at once?" she asked. She reached the bottle out to Otto. He looked at it glistening in the moonlight. The rushing sound of the river seemed to grow louder in the silence that hung on Celia's question.

"Probably at least *eight* bottles," Celia concluded.

The thought hit Otto like a pile of bricks.

Keen made a small chirping noise, something between a gasp of terror and a whimper of defeat. Otto's body shuttered under the weight of the idea. Then his shoulders slumped, and he let out a huge breath.

"Eight bottles?" he asked, defeated.

"Easily," Celia replied. "Maybe even more, if I could find something to carry them in."

"*Carry them in?*" Otto repeated weakly. He reached out and grasped the almost-empty bottle from Celia. Then he began to cradle it like an infant in his arms.

"For the love of frog eggs and all things fishy…" he whispered to himself and the bottle. He turned to Keen. His mind was firmly made.

"We have no choice," Otto said. "I am so low on reserves. So very, very low. Remember what happened last time I ran out completely?"

They both paused and looked away from each other, lost in an unpleasant memory that Celia could only imagine.

"And with eight bottles in one run…" Otto's eyes began to glisten. A switch had flipped in his brain and there was no turning back now.

"This could help me stock up for the long months when the humans shut down the habitat," Otto calculated. Keen shook his head slowly. He was trying to think of something to refute this idea.

"But with more bottles to drink, there will be more risk of

trouble…" Keen said, letting his voice trail off.

"No," Otto said with conviction. "With fewer trips for replenishing, there will be less risk of getting caught."

"More risk of trouble," said Keen

"Less!"

"More!"

"Less!"

"I will NOT help if it means more bottles!" Keen suddenly exploded, feathers falling from his puffed neck and wings. The two animals stood staring at each other, equally shocked by Keen's defiance. He was panting heavily as if he had just released something—the fear and love for his friend—the desperation to avoid something terrible he has witnessed repeatedly for some time now.

Celia stood in the silence between the two friends. She realized it was Keen's wings that would cover the ground needed to find Tippit, and Otto's swimming that would bring her to the Snapping Turtle King. She needed both of them. She quickly thought over the little she knew of Keen's character, and although she wouldn't be proud of it later, she calculated the perfect lie.

"But, Keen…" she said slowly, turning to the tiny bird, "Tippit needs your *help*. She is in *danger* and I need to *protect* her."

"Danger?" Keen said, the little, tufted feathers on his ears perking up as he turned his head.

"Oh, yes," Celia said. "I need to warn her. To keep her *safe*."

"What kind of danger?" Keen asked, immediately intrigued.

"Big danger!" Celia said. "She needs your *protection!*"

"Protection?" Keen's chest puffed out. His little beak rose in the air. "From what?" he asked. He couldn't help himself.

Celia quickly said whatever came to her mind first. "Anayla and her pack!" she explained. "The wolves are out to get Tippit."

Both Keen and Otto shivered at Anayla's name.

"But how could I protect anyone from Anayla?" Keen asked looking doubtful.

"You are the fiercest animal I have met in the woods!" Celia insisted. "I have never seen such swift flying, or ruthless use of beak and talon. I have faced Anayla and her pack and lived to tell the tale without a scratch on my body...but *you*? Well..."

Celia turned her head to show the dried trickle of blood at the nape of her neck, "...I rest my case," she finished.

By the time she was finished speaking, Keen's chest feathers were so puffed out that he looked almost twice his original girth.

"You met Anayla and lived to tell the tale?" Otto asked with an eyebrow raised.

"Yes," Celia said, lifting her chin, trying to make herself a little taller.

"I will *help* you!" Keen suddenly screeched out, rising into the air by the force of his own excitement. "I will find the fox named Tippit and bring her to you so that we can *protect* her!"

Celia turned to Otto with a sigh of relief. "And you will bring me to the Snapping Turtle King?" she asked.

"For eight bottles," Otto nodded, with a strange, faraway expression on his face.

"Excellent!" Celia said. "It's a deal! Shake?" They all shook hands, paws, and wings, agreeing to return to the same place the next night. Then Celia disappeared back through the bushes.

Both animals stared blankly at the swish in the undergrowth long after she was gone. Besides the trickle of the river, everything was still again. Keen felt the sneaking suspicion that he had just somehow been tricked. He fended off the feeling by immediately busying himself with a meticulous grooming of his wing feathers. Otto, however, still in some sort of trance, stared at the moonlight dancing on the water's surface, thinking of nothing, absolutely nothing, but eight great big, shining bottles filled with the sharp, magical liquid that always wiped away all his sadness inside.

24. A New Deal

Raindrops pelted against the tin roof of the Cupcake. The dripping wind whipped through the screens, sending Mrs. Nalgy scurrying around to shut the glass windows. Instantly, everything became so warm and steamy, she scurried around again to reopen them.

As the clouds outside the Cupcake rumbled with thunder, inside Celia grumbled silently with boredom. She pretended to sleep the whole morning and afternoon as she listened to the shrieks of girls splashing down the flooded paths. She felt a strong longing to join the laughter and wet slapping of bare feet in the mud, but she needed to hold up her part of the deal with Otto and Keen. And in order to do that, she needed one more night in the Cupcake.

Just before sunset, the rain lifted and the clouds opened to display a beautiful, sharp pink sky. Celia cracked her eyes and peeked out the window. The world looked vibrantly bright, as if a sheen of weariness had been washed away, and everything was sparkling new. The golden sunlight streaked through the trees catching the rainwater on every leaf, blade of grass, upturned flower, even the soil itself, and set them glowing. Lightning bugs, crickets and cicadas came out in full force. There were distant muffled voices of laughter and singing as the girls gathered in the Chow Lodge for dinner.

Then, as if the excitement of the day's storm had worn out both Mother Nature and humans alike, the sky quickly darkened, the girls headed back to their dorms, and a silence nestled over the camp long before the moon began to rise.

Celia waited patiently as Mrs. Nalgy drank her nightly mug of peppermint tea, rolled her hair into curlers, and tucked herself into her cot. Knowing that this would be her last night in the Cupcake, Celia relished listening to Mrs. Nalgy's normal breathing slow and transform into the soft snoring which she now found comforting.

When all was still, Celia climbed out of bed, carefully lifted the kitchen clock aside, and used the hidden keys to unlock the medicine cabinet. She inspected one of the bottles. *Rubbing Alcohol.* She flipped the bottle over and read the back label. *"Warning: Do not ingest! Even smallest amounts can lead to blindness or death."*

Celia's heart sunk. Blindness? Death? How could she knowingly give this poison to Otto? She grabbed three bottles, instead of eight, and pushed the others to the front to make the cabinet look full again. After locking the cabinet, she replaced the key behind the clock.

Celia snuck out of the screen door, and back into the woods to where the river ran. It was much larger today, swollen from the storm's rainwater. She stood and stared at the swift, rushing, churning, dark current.

Celia couldn't help but imagine what it would be like to drown in a river like this. It must be like suddenly finding yourself trapped underneath a tilting, clear glass wall that's pressing down on you in an airless room, where you are unable to scream or move, as you watch the world, everyone and everything you know, slowly recede into darkness.

Then, forcefully shaking the thought from her head, Celia knelt at the water's edge and dipped her hands into the stream. She reached out to anyone or anything that might be trapped beneath the current. Stinging cramps shot up from the frigid water to her palms and forearms, but despite the burning cold, she pushed her hands deeper. She left them there, wavering aimlessly in the powerful water. She breathed deeply into the pain, waiting. But nothing reached out to take her hands. Finally, she cupped her stiff hands, and splashed some water onto her face. She sputtered and wiped the falling droplets away from her eyes, peering into the cold, unforgiving current.

I am not afraid of you, she said to it.

Then she heard a rustling in the underbrush. Before Otto and Keen reached her, Celia could see they were alone.

"Where's Tippit?" she asked.

"Couldn't find her," Otto yelled back, hopping across slick rocks to join her.

"I flew across every hill, and back into the valley," reported Keen, landing gently on the ground beside Otto. "We asked other birds, chipmunks, squirrels, a family of raccoons, even a grey fox. No one knew where to find her," he said sheepishly tucking his wings behind him.

"Did you at least find her den?" Celia asked.

"I did. And you were right. Anayla and her pack were there, lounging around outside it," Keen said.

"They *were*?" Celia asked, surprised by the coincidence.

"Looking terrible and fierce," Otto confirmed with a shudder.

"Yes. But we saw no signs of the fox. I hope we're not too late," Keen finished quietly, nodding his head to one side.

"It is very peculiar though," Otto added, feverishly eyeing the bottles by Celia's side, "because I swear I can *smell* a fox everywhere…"

"Well, then we don't have a deal," Celia said, disappointed not to see Tippit, but also relieved that she wouldn't have to give Otto the poison.

"Not so fast!" Otto shot a pointed claw into the air. "I will still take you to…" Otto paused and looked around carefully, as if he expected someone or something to be watching them. He muttered under his breath, and motioned for Keen and Celia to move closer.

They did.

"I will still take you to the Snapping Turtle King," he whispered. "That's half the deal, and it looks like, coincidentally, you only brought less than half the bottles you promised anyway," he added, eyeing Celia's load.

"Ok, deal," Celia said, "We'll leave the bottles here with Keen. You bring me to the Snapping Turtle King, and when we return, you can keep the bottles," she said.

"Right…" Otto said slowly, "When we return…" he said nodding. Suddenly, his conscience got the better of him. "Celia," he said, his hazel eyes softened, "I don't think you understand the risk this is for you…"

"Is it true that he can speak with the dead?" Celia interrupted his impending speech.

Otto nodded. He drew in a deep breath. "I've gone to him a few times to speak to my father." Keen turned to Otto with a look of surprise. Otto shrugged and continued. "The Snapping Turtle King has told me things that would be impossible for him to know otherwise. But you are different. You are a human, and a Speaker, no less."

"Do you think he can speak to my brother?" Celia asked, determination rising inside her chest.

"It's *possible*," Otto said.

"Well, then it is worth the risk."

"Sure, but what if…" Keen began to say.

"FOR THE LOVE OF ALL THINGS CLAWED AND CARNIVOROUS!" Otto suddenly yelled, startled by something behind Celia. He jumped into the air, then dove clear into the river.

In the next instant, Keen saw whatever Otto had seen, and frantically shot into the air, crashed into a low-hanging tree branch, and plummeted back to the ground, completely knocked out cold.

Celia whirled around and saw a full-grown fox standing behind her.

"Tippit!" she cried.

25. Reunion

Celia and Tippit stared at each other for a moment, shocked by the sudden and dramatic nature of Otto and Keen's exits. Then Celia shook her head and came to her senses.

"Tippit! What are you doing here?" she yelled, feeling both surprised and relieved to see her friend.

"Celia, don't go to the Snapping Turtle King," Tippit pleaded in a calm, steady voice.

At that moment, Keen woke up with a feather-fluffing twitter, and immediately began dive-bombing Tippit at close range.

"Keen!" Celia yelled. "Stop! It's okay!" but he couldn't hear her over the sound of his own screeching. Tippit snapped her teeth once or twice at the frantic bird, but quickly realized the effort was futile. She sheltered her head miserably under her front paws, and thrashed her tail back and forth while Keen continued to dive-bomb her. A familiar cursing grew louder and then joined the fray as Otto clawed his way out of the river.

"THAT WILL DO, KEEN!" Otto called, and just like last time, Keen halted mid-air and fluttered gracefully to the forest floor. Otto glared at Tippit who was peeking her snout out from under her paws. Then he busied himself by shaking the water out of his ears.

"Did I do good? Did I? Did I get the fox? Did I protect you?"

Celia realized that Keen was talking to her this time.

"Keen, this is who you were supposed to *find*!" Celia said to the little bird. "This is my friend, Tippit."

Keen's chest was puffing up and down, up and down. His eyes were as wide as quarters.

"It is?" he asked. He turned his head in a complete half rotation without moving his body to get a better look at the fox.

"How did you find us?" Celia asked Tippit.

Tippit bowed her head, as if embarrassed. "I've been following you since the night we parted," she said.

Otto grumbled. "See? What did I *tell* you? *'A Speaker, a liar, and add stupidity to the mix!?'* I *knew* that you weren't alone," he grumbled. "I could smell that fox the first time we met. Even caught a glimpse of her once by the Lake, but then when you asked us to find her, we couldn't!" He turned his glare to Tippit, "Where've you been hiding, anyway?"

Tippit stared at Otto and said nothing.

"OH, FOR THE LOVE OF LIGHTNING BOLTS AND SUDDEN SQUALLS!" he yelled. "Give it up! Where were you?"

"I've been under the floorboards of the human habitat where Celia was resting," she said in a quiet voice.

"You were under the Cupcake?!" Celia asked.

"Poppycock and bull feathers!" Otto blustered. "We were under there last night!"

"Well, I smelled you coming from half a mile away," Tippit said as she wrapped her tail neatly around her paws and stared back at them, "and I made myself a discreet hiding spot."

"A hiding spot?" Otto sputtered, skeptically.

"Foxes are excellent burrowers," Tippit said, "and if you didn't know that before, you do now."

Otto just rolled his eyes and muttered something completely inaudible to the sky.

Keen busied himself with ruffling his feathers and muttering something about he himself never going under the human habitat, *that* was Otto's domain.

Tippit winked at Celia. Celia winked back.

Then she rushed forward and gave Tippit a big hug and buried her nose into her soft, brushy fur.

"I'm so sorry I got angry with you and said those nasty things," Celia gushed.

"I'm sorry I couldn't help you in the way that you needed," Tippit said looking down at her paws.

"No, you *did* help me," Celia said. "You helped me face the truth that Kyel is gone."

"I know, Celia. I spoke to the Lynx after you ran away."

"You went into the cave?" Celia asked, thinking about all the fox skulls she had seen in there.

"He was surprisingly kind, and thankfully not hungry," Tippit said. "But he told me about Kyel." The fox bowed her head. "Celia, I am so sorry."

Celia hugged Tippit again, and the fox nuzzled her head into Celia's arms.

"Thank you," Celia whispered softly into Tippit's ear.

"You're welcome," Tippit said, looking pleased. "And I... ummmm... I brought you this." Tippit uncovered a limp, dead mouse from a pile of leaves. "You must be hungry."

Celia felt her stomach lurch as she looked at the unfortunate tiny creature's hair matted with blood. She smiled at Tippit bravely.

"Thank you, but I'm alright," she said.

Keen, however, eyed the mouse with a very interested quiver in his beak.

A thought occurred to Celia.

"If you have been with me this whole time, who's been feeding the kits?" she asked.

"Anayla's pack has been caring for them, bringing them food and protecting the den." Both Otto and Keen shuddered at the mention of Anayla's name.

"You tricked us!" Keen piped up. "There was never any danger," he said. Celia felt a pang of guilt.

"I'm sorry," she said ruffling his feathers affectionately. "I just didn't know what else to do to get your help."

"Well, there's plenty of danger ahead to make up for it," Otto mumbled.

"Yes…about that," Tippit said looking at Celia, "please reconsider going to the Snapping Turtle King," she begged. "He is not to be trusted."

Celia looked at Tippit with pleading eyes.

"I need to see if the Snapping Turtle King can speak to Kyel."

Tippit closed her eyes, and took a deep breath.

"Well, if your mind is already made up, then I'm coming with you."

"What?" Otto snorted. "Foxes can't swim!"

Tippit turned an annoyed eye towards the otter. "Apparently," she said, "there is *plenty* you don't know about foxes. We *can* swim, and I just so happen to be aquatically exceptional …for a fox."

Celia looked at Tippit. "I'm not sure if it's a good idea," she said, not wanting to drag her friend into a dangerous situation.

"I insist," Tippit said, and Celia shrugged and smiled, knowing that there was no use in arguing with a stubborn fox.

Otto simply shook his head.

"Fine," he grumbled. "But let's get one thing straight; when we get to the Palace, I do the talking."

Both Celia and Tippit nodded.

"A reasonable compromise," Tippit said.

"Alright..." Otto said, and he began hobbling towards the water. "Let's get moving! Celia, shoes off. Keen, guard the bottles. Fox..." (here Otto just rolled his eyes...) "We're off!" he yelled as he motioned toward the water.

Celia followed Otto's directions, quickly slipping out of her red Keds sneakers. Keen looked slightly miserable about being left behind, but he too followed Otto's orders and nested down into one of Celia's shoes. Tippit stretched her haunches, then nudged the dead mouse towards Keen. The bird instantly cheered up as he tugged at one of the limp paws with his beak.

Otto pulled an empty glass bottle from the thick reeds growing by the water. He handed it to Celia.

"This will act as an extra lung for you," he said. "You're going to need it."

26. The Dive

Celia and Tippit followed Otto along the bank of the river until it reached the Lake's edge. At the edge of the water Celia could see the Ducky Hut off in the distance. Its low-sloping roof shone in the moonlight. The sailboats were moored in a bobbing line. They looked like sleeping butterflies with their sails folded against the masts.

Celia followed Otto into the thick reeds with Tippit trotting close behind them. Cold, wet mud pushed into the cracks between Celia's toes. Her teeth began to chatter and her muscles cramped, shooting icicles up her calves, and behind her kneecaps. She took a deep breath and waded into the water up to her shins, then her waist.

Otto was beside her, now totally submerged in water, his limping hobble gone. He moved with speed and grace, like a younger otter pup, as if he had shed years off his life gliding into the water. Behind her, Tippit slunk into the water. She splashed behind them, using a simple doggy-paddle to keep up. It wasn't exactly quiet or graceful, but it was fast and efficient.

The three swam with their heads above the water out into the middle of the large Lake. Otto swam beside Celia as if flying, turning and rolling onto his back, leading them deeper and deeper into the water. Celia looked back at Tippit. With her wet fur matted against her skin, she looked much smaller, only a smidge bigger than

Otto, really. She swam with her nose pointed towards the sky and a strained grimace in her eyes.

"All ok?" Celia called to her.

"Never been better," Tippit said, trying to fake a smile.

Celia felt her own body warming up as she pumped and pulled her arms and legs. She watched the moonlight dancing on the moving water, and she felt like it was her own body crackling with nervous energy. After continuing in silence a bit longer, a question popped into her racing mind. She looked over at Otto.

"How did you and Keen meet?" she asked.

"Lightning bolt strike," he answered, turning onto his back and looking up at the stars.

"Like love?" Celia asked.

"No," Otto said calmly, without ceasing to swim, "a lightning bolt from the sky struck the tree where his family nested. The tree, along with his family, was incinerated. He was the only one to survive. I found him burnt half to a crisp, but still fighting to hang on. He is a natural fighter; a quality I quite admire." Otto paused, and shot a quick glance at Celia. "I nursed him back to health, and well... we never saw a reason to part after that."

"Oh," Celia said softly. "That's sad," she said, "and beautiful." Sad and beautiful, she thought. What an interesting combination.

Then Otto gruffly added, "Don't get me wrong. There was certainly love involved, but I was just...in that sentence... referring to an actual lightning bolt," he said.

"I understand," Celia said, feeling somewhat honored that Otto would tell her this. Then she asked him, "What about you? Where is your family?" Otto abruptly rolled over onto his belly and his mood darkened.

"Not everything is your business to know," he answered.

"Oh, sorry," Celia muttered half underwater.

They swam the rest of the way without speaking. The only noise on the Lake was Tippit's soft splashing, and an occasional grunt of effort from her behind them.

When they reached the center of the Lake, at the point farthest away from any shoreline, the water suddenly became colder, as if there was a large drop below them. The color of the water reflecting in the moonlight also grew much, much darker turning from an emerald green to a deep amber brown. Dread slowly slipped from Celia's subconscious to the forefront of her mind, chilling her thoughts and heart.

"Deep, deep breath now, Celia," Otto said. "Cover the opening of the bottle with your thumb. You will need the extra air to get there."

"Is it that far?" she asked, doubt creeping into her voice.

Otto twitched his whiskers at Celia, as if making some calculations. "Trust me; you can make it," he said, and suddenly dove. Tippit took a large breath, and in a flash of dripping orangey-red, she was gone.

Celia watched the ripples on the surface expand around where both animals had just vanished. She quickly took three large gulps of air, put her thumb over the bottle's mouth and dove straight down.

Celia swam. She closed her eyes and let her mind go blank while she focused on fighting against the rising pull to the surface. Despite the cold, her thrashing legs soon began to feel as if they were burning. The red hot sensation quickly traveled to her arms, her chest, and then her head. She opened her eyes and saw that the moon was now just a tiny watery marble drifting further and further away. The water was getting darker and colder with every giant stroke of her powerful arms. Celia began to feel a lightness filling her head. It was such a peaceful feeling. So wonderful. *Is this how the bottles make Otto feel?* she wondered. If so, it now made sense. She looked ahead of her. Otto was fading into a fuzzy blur.

Suddenly Tippit's bright orange-red face was directly in front of hers. Tippit nudged Celia's arm and pushed the bottle of air toward her lips. Celia put her mouth over the bottle's opening and inhaled a small breath of air. It had a sour, tangy taste, but her vision cleared. She focused on Tippit's shimmering golden eyes. She motioned to Celia with two waving paws to carry on. Celia took another large gasp of air, and with five powerful strokes of her arms, plummeted to the lowest depth of the dark body of water.

The water at the bottom of the Lake was very still. This mud had not been disturbed for decades. Celia fought a strange urge to lie down on the Lake's murky floor and settle into the cool, soft mud and stare up at the gentle, distant flicker of the moonlight above. It would be the absolute opposite of warming herself by a fireplace, but what peace she would feel. Everything would be still and quiet, perfect and forever the same. There would be no distractions or bad news for the rest of her life, barely any sound at all – just a faint echo coming through the water from far, far away. She would never have another person she loved taken from her. If she just stayed here, she would never have to feel sad – or really feel anything else at all – ever again.

This time Otto pulled on Celia's arm. He looked deep into her eyes and saw the sadness resting there. He shook his head and pulled her arm to swim forward. As they glided through the water, Celia began to make out large figures looming ahead. At first she thought about the rock figures outside of the Lynx's cave. Then she saw that buried deep in the mud and rotting leaves and twigs, were the towering remains of large, ancient trees. Celia realized that this must have been a forest, long before beavers came and built a dam, which created the Lake.

Curiously, in front of Otto, a new faint light began to glow, coming from something just beyond them. Celia took another gulp of sour air from the bottle and swam toward it. As the three swam closer to the massive structures, Celia could see faint lights within the trees. Otto motioned for Celia and Tippit to follow him through their twisted, gnarled root-structures, which were both as beautiful and mysterious as the veins in an old woman's hands. Finally, they arrived at the largest tree in the underwater forest. Otto led Tippit and Celia through a grandly ornate entrance made of entwined underwater plants. They glided into a watery tunnel that tilted upward.

Suddenly, with a swoosh of bubbles, Otto's head disappeared. Then Tippit's. Finally, Celia's head splashed through the water's surface into a large, airy chamber. All three of them gulped large lungfuls of air, and treaded the cold water, panting to regain their breath. Their coughs, bellowing breaths, and sighs of relief, echoed through the hollowed chamber of the petrified tree.

"Phew!" Tippit gasped, giving Celia a sideways glance, "I thought I'd lost you for a moment."

Celia shook a braid away from her face.

"Nah," she said, "we made it."

"Well done, Celia," Otto said placing a careful paw on her shoulder. There was a new air of respect in his tone. "Seems like you've got that fighter's quality in you, too," he said.

Celia felt a tingle of pride, but she turned away, pretending to be busy looking at what surrounded them. Otto set his sights on the dark hallway before them.

"Alright!" he said, with a twinkle in his eye. "Let's see what the Snapping Turtle King can do for us tonight!"

27. The Snapping Turtle King

Celia, Otto and Tippit crawled out of the water and up a steep sloping bank that was slick with dark green algae. Celia gazed around her. Somehow, tiny air bubbles had leaked through small shafts in the mud to fill this hollowed trunk, making it a place where those who breathe air, but don't seek the sun, may dwell.

What kind of creature would want to live down here, Celia wondered, *so tucked away from sunlight and anything living?* But even as she asked herself the question, she thought about her own feelings on the dive down, and realized that she already knew the answer.

Once they reached even ground, Tippit hung behind the other two for a moment. With a vigorous whole-body shake, followed by an unapologetic spray of water droplets, she poofed back to her normal size. Then she trotted to catch up with Celia and Otto who were already progressing down a long hallway that was lit on both sides by dim, glimmering lanterns.

Celia stopped to peer into one of the lanterns. She discovered they weren't lit with fire, but rather held pools of water swarming with glowing fish and unusual creatures with lop-sided faces and bulging eyes which gave off just enough yellowish-green light to cast shadows down the hallway.

At the end of the hallway they reached two massive doors covered with detailed carvings of underwater plants. Otto rang a large bell hanging on the wall, and slowly the doors swung open revealing the Great Hall of the Snapping Turtle Palace. Celia stood gazing, her mouth agape.

Sections of turtle shells tiled the expansive floor. The rafters of the vaulted ceiling above her head were decorated with complex patterns of turtle skulls and bones stacked upon each other. Looking around, Celia noticed that the walls were not really walls. They were four solid lines of Snapping Turtles standing guard, heavily armored by their shells. The real walls were several paces behind them.

At the other side of the great room was a throne. It was an intricate structure made of the shells and cleanly picked bones of snapping turtles. It sat inside a small archway made entirely from the sharp, curved pointed beaks, and hollow, dark eye sockets of snapping turtle skulls.

Seated under the archway and on top of the throne was the largest, oldest turtle Celia had ever seen, breathing heavily through rasping lungs that rose and collapsed deep inside his chest.

It was the Snapping Turtle King.

The King's head extended on a long snake-like neck. Atop it rested a crown made of long, thin fangs. His beady, blood red eyes were pinpricked with tiny pitch black centers. And his shell was different from any other turtle Celia had ever seen warming itself on sun-drenched logs in the city's parks. It was not smooth and round. Instead it was covered with huge pyramid-like spikes that ran down his back in multiple rows. The King's tough, thick skin was covered in similar tiny spikes, but peeling and flaking off in curling strips. His feet and arms were webbed and tipped with long, butter-yellow claws that looked as sharp as daggers.

"Enter!" a voice rang out, causing Tippit and Celia to jump. Otto, however, hunched lower to the floor, and began to advance forward with a wily glint in his eyes. Tippit and Celia entered the great hall a few steps behind him. Its smell was strong, sharp, and fishy. Once the three had passed through the threshold of the room, the large doors slammed shut behind them. Besides the sound of water dripping quietly somewhere in a dark corner, the large chamber was silent.

Celia felt every eye in the Great Hall follow them as they passed row after row of guards. They approached the throne cautiously and stopped at a safe enough distance. The King's tiny red eyes glared fiercely at Otto, but did not seem to notice Tippit or Celia, who stood a few paces behind him.

"Your majesty..." Otto said now on one knee with his head bowed low.

"Sssssilencccccce!" the King hissed. The sound of his voice shot barbed wire through Celia's veins. "I told you not to return for two full-moonssssss," he said.

"Your majesty," Otto began again, "I am here to ..." his voice was threaded with a slight quiver.

"I care not!" the King yelled. "I gave you clear insssssssstructions, you disgusssting, addicted, greedy, filthy disssgraccce, NOT to return until two full moons!"

Otto winced and crouched smaller and smaller with every accusatory word. His shoulders slumped and his whiskers drooped.

"But I am not here to..." Otto began, but the King cut him off instantly.

"Your dead father does NOT WISH TO SPEAK TO YOU!" the King yelled. The words rang out and echoed against every surface inside the chamber. The guards looked at the King with trepidation, but he quickly regained his composure. "Get that through your thick, pathetic sssskull," he spat.

Celia stared at Otto's face as it crumbled into disappointment. His little mouth hung open, as if he would make one last attempt, but nothing came out.

"Take him," the King said with a flat, calm voice and a sweeping motion of his claws. Immediately two guards stepped forward and grabbed Otto's arms.

"Wait! Your majesty!" Celia yelled, stepping forward.

The guards froze.

The King reeled around and weaved his head forward on his long, serpentine neck. His red eyes focused in the dim light, seeing Tippit and Celia for the first time. He looked them over carefully, immediately dismissing the fox, and focusing entirely on Celia. Relaxing his squinted eyes, the Snapping Turtle King's mouth curled slightly with recognition.

"Sssssssssssssssssssssssssssspeaker..." he hissed.

A rumbling of muffled words spread between the guards.

"SILENCE!" the King yelled, and all was silent except for the water dripping quietly somewhere in a dark corner.

"Sssssssssssspeaker child," the King whispered to himself, as if turning over the burning ember of an idea as he decided whether to fan or smother it.

After a moment of thought, a long, terrifying smile spread across his face. The King gave a small gesture with a single clawed finger and the guards released Otto. Otto smoothed his ruffled fur where the guards had held him, but remained uncharacteristically silent.

"Dessssspicible addict," the King grunted, before he turned his focus back to Celia.

"Sssssssooooo," he said. He folded his webbed hands in his lap. "To what do I owe thisss pleasure...thisss HONOR... this unexpected visssit from a Sssssssssspeaker?" he asked. "Why do you graccce my humble Palace with your humanly presenccce? Whatever could I, such a lowly creature, do for you, a fine human of such extraordinary oratorical talentsss?"

Celia chose her next words as if she was crossing a tightrope in the dark.

"Great King," she began. "I am here because..."

"Shhhhhhhhhh..." the King whispered. He extended a single claw and beckoned to her. "Come clossssser, my dear. I am very, very old, and don't hear as well as I once did."

Celia took a few steps closer to the throne. He motioned with the single claw for her to proceed closer and closer until she was standing directly in front of the Snapping Turtle King. Tippit followed just a few steps behind her.

"Intriguing," the King murmured to himself, watching the fox with a raised brow.

Standing right before him now, Celia fought to keep her breath regular. The King was even more hideous up close. His wide, powerful mouth remained slightly ajar, like a spring trap poised to snap. His jawbone hooked down into a sharp point at the middle with a piercing tip that could easily puncture her skull. A dank, murky smell wafted from his skin where it sagged away from the hollow spaces inside his shell.

"Ssssssssspeak, human child," he said. "Ssssssssssspeak."

"Your majesty," Celia said, her voice now wavering with fear. The King closed his eyes and his tongue flickered in and out of his mouth.

"I have heard of your powers," she began, "to speak with those who have died."

"Oh?" the King interrupted her with mock surprise. He opened his eyes and lightly touched a clawed hand to his chest. "Has news traveled so far?" he asked.

Celia nodded. Fear, like she had never felt before, was building up in her chest.

"Issssssssss there sssssssssssomeone with whom you wisssssshhhhhhhh to sssssspeak?" he asked.

"Yes," Celia whispered. She thought of Kyel and tried to gather her courage. She pressed her leg against Tippit's warm fur huddled against her, but she still felt the fear washing over her.

"Well…?" the King asked raising his crusty eyelids, waiting for Celia to speak.

But she could not.

She was frozen with fear – fear of this creature before her, but also fear of facing her brother. What if the Snapping Turtle King *could* speak to Kyel? What would she say to him? And more terrifyingly, what would he say to her?

The King narrowed his eyes in the proceeding silence. The guards shifted uncomfortably and watched closely.

The King sat on his throne for another quarter of a minute staring at Celia. Then, without any trace of a smile, he slunk off his seat and approached her. She felt Tippit's body begin to shiver as the long claws on the King's webbed feet made a clicking, clacking sound as they dragged slowly across the floor. He circled Celia twice, then stopping again directly in front of her. He brought the sharp point of his mouth very close to her ear.

"Do not wassste my time, Sssssspeaker," he whispered. "I

already know why you are here, and I have absssolutely no intention of helping you. In fact, quite the oppossite." He pulled away from her ear and brought his eyes level with hers, and smiled a deep, tortured smile.

Celia's mind was entirely frozen. She gasped quietly for breath through slightly parted lips, unable to think or respond.

"I do not believe you!" Tippit suddenly barked into the silent hall. It was the first time she had spoken since they arrived at the Palace, and all eyes, including Otto's and Celia's, turned toward her with surprise.

"WHAT?!" the Snapping Turtle King snarled, looking down towards the crouching fox.

"I... I don't believe that you can do it, your majesty...I mean, speak with Celia's brother," Tippit spoke again as loudly as she could in her trembling voice. "He...he is a human, after all, and you have never proven that you can speak to humans. Animals...s-sure. But not h-humans..." Tippit's voice tapered off into a shivering silence. Celia gaped at Tippit with shock.

The Snapping Turtle King narrowed his eyes and glared at Tippit. A low rumble of fury, an almost painful sounding growl, came from deep in his throat as he stared at her. Then he faced the room full of his guards, who looked at him with blank expressions, watching his every move to see what would happen next.

He turned to Celia, who was still unable to speak.

"You've traveled from over a hundred miles away," he began quickly. "You came to our woods looking for sssssssssssomeone who..." he paused and licked the sharp point of his beak. "Sssssssssssomeone who you said was missssssssssssing." His leathery lips curled. Celia felt her blood quicken.

"But!" the King continued, whirling around, now addressing the whole chamber of guards, "you knew he wasssssssss dead." He pointed a yellow, curling claw at Celia. "A deccceitful liar!" he hissed. "A coward!"

Something in this accusation freed Celia from her moment of paralysis. Tippit had gotten her this far, she thought. She needed to take the lead.

"Who was it?" Celia croaked. It took all of her courage to force the three words. The Snapping Turtle King paused and looked around the top rafters of the Great Hall. He waved his head from side to side, as if listening for something.

"He was your kin. A younger male."

"What else?" Celia asked hoarsely.

"Let me sssssseeeeeee," the King said, stroking his chin, closing his eyes.

"Yessssss...it happened just over three full moonsssssss now. The boy had magnificent dark skin like yours, slightly shorter in stature, only slightly though...strong arms and high cheek bones... but a very, very weak swimmer." A murmur of disapproval rolled through the guards.

"He was so frightened," the King continued, "...as he drowned...he was crying, no whimpering really...if you can even do that underwater. Very pitiful and weak, your kind," the King said with a disgusted shake of his head. Then he opened his eyes.

"Half of the woods, and any one of your soldier spies could have told you that!" Celia suddenly yelled. The defiance in her voice filled the room. The guards could hear it clearly, although what they couldn't hear, since they were so unaccustomed to its sound, was the hope that was also rising in her chest.

"Fine," the King said slowly, recognizing the challenge presented before him. "Ask me about something no other creature in the woods would know." Celia thought for a moment. Then she asked the simplest thing that came to her mind.

"What is my brother's middle name?" she asked. She was certain that she had not told this to anyone since coming to Camp Glynwood or the woods.

The guards shifted uncomfortably.

"Hhhhhmmmmmmm…" The Snapping Turtle King began to hum. He closed his eyes.

Celia held her breath. The King wavered on his legs, and facing upward, weaved his long neck back and forth, and reached one hand out as if he could feel something just beyond his terrible claws.

"What is your middle name, boy?" he whispered in a dreadful, cold voice that was different from the way he spoke before.

There was a long silence in return. Tippit and Otto stared at the King. Not a single guard appeared to breathe.

"Kyel…" the Snapping Turtle King finally said.

"Kyel was his first name!" Celia yelled, disappointment and anger filling her and her clenched fists. But the King's eyes were still closed.

"Kyel Kingston Johnson," he said in the same sunken voice. Then he opened his red eyes and looked straight at Celia. "What kind of middle name is Kingsssssssssssssston?"

Celia's mouth dropped open. She stared directly at the King, the blood drained from her face. Seeing her expression, the King just smiled, sadly.

"How do you know that?" she whispered.

"I know, because it's my gift, and my curse," he answered. Grief suddenly filled his own eyes.

"Tell Kyel I'm here!" Celia said desperately. "Tell him I love him!"

The King shook his head quietly, and didn't say a thing.

"Say it!" Celia yelled. The guards breathed in a collective gasp, audibly nervous for the King's impending reaction. But the King remained silent for a long time. He looked tired, and older, and sadder than before. His arms rested at his sides and he stared ahead without focusing on anything.

Celia felt like she was caught in one of her nightmares where Kyel was just beyond her fingertips, at the building's edge or out on the tree limb, unable to hear her screams. She looked up into the rafters of the Great Hall.

"KYEL!" she screamed. "CAN YOU HEAR ME?" Her voice echoed around the nooks and crannies of all the bones, but the Snapping Turtle King just stared at her. Tippit, Otto and all the guards watched with large eyes. Silence followed. Then just as quickly as it had appeared, the King's sadness was buried again under the return of his rage.

The Snapping Turtle King threw his head back and began to laugh a terrible, wicked laugh, filled with anger and despair.

"Let's go, Celia," Otto said, appearing at Celia's side, tugging her arm and turning away. "We will find no mercy here."

But Celia could not turn away. She watched as the King laughed at her, laughed at her pain, laughed at Kyel's death. She was so close to speaking with Kyel. He was there somewhere, but she couldn't reach him. Before she could control herself, she sprang forward and struck the Snapping Turtle King across his leathery face.

28. A Reminder of Sunlight

In a flash the Snapping Turtle King grabbed both of Celia's hands and held them above her head, lifting her off the floor with surprising strength. The entire mass of guards rushed forward with a deafening noise so that the room itself shrunk significantly. Guards grabbed Tippit and Otto, dragging them away from Celia who dangled helplessly above the floor, her feet kicking harmlessly at the air around her.

The Snapping Turtle King stretched his jaw where she had struck him. He opened and closed it, and shifted it from side to side. The King was looking Celia over—deciding whether he should tear both her arms off right then, or kill her more slowly—when the baggy sleeves of her Dodgers sweatshirt fell to her elbows. A flicker of light caught the King's attention. Something sparkling hung on Celia's wrist. It was Violet's prism, still tied tightly. The Snapping Turtle King's face twisted into an expression of curiosity.

"What is thissssssss?" he asked, using his snake-like neck to move his eyes closer to the object on her wrist.

"It's…it's a prism," Celia managed to stammer while still dangling. "It's my friend's," she said. The King looked at it with fascination. He brought her feet back to the floor, still holding her wrists, and tugged roughly at her arms to bring the prism closer to his terrifying, red eyes.

"What does it do?" he asked.

"It makes rainbows out of sunlight," she said.

The King continued to stare at the prism. He was silent for a long time.

"Ssssssunlight?" he said quietly to himself as he twisted her wrist uncomfortably to get a better look. His tongue flicked the air around the prism, as if to help him understand it better.

"The beams of light reflect..." Celia began.

"Sssssssshhhhhhhhhh..." the King interrupted her, "I know what it does."

He took one claw and slipped it under the leather. Celia thought that he would use the sharp claw to snap the prism off her wrist, but instead, he just turned it this way and that, staring into the many cuts and folds inside the plastic. His claw began to tremble. Then his whole body was shaking. He let go of Celia's wrists and staggered one step backward, looking at her with a new, bewildered stare. Celia rubbed her wrists where he had held her. The skin felt particularly cold.

The Snapping Turtle King stumbled backward a few more steps and then sunk into his throne. He closed his eyes and rested his head in one of his hands.

"Do you know who enjoyed the ssssssunlight?" he asked, loud enough to address the whole hall. He opened his eyes and stared at Celia.

The question hovered, unanswered in the damp air.

"MY QUEEN!" he yelled suddenly, slamming a heavy fist into

the armrest of his throne.

"Years and years and years ago, we used to live in the warm sssssunlight...me and my beautiful, loving, courageous, nurturing, brave Queen. But no longer! And do you know WHY?" he yelled. Celia stood frozen, unable to move.

"Because she was TAKEN from me... from us... murdered by a Sssspeaker." He opened his eyes wider and looked at his guards. Most of them were kneeling now. He continued speaking louder. "For years, and years, I have been driven mad by the sssound of her weeping, the echoesss of her sssorrow. She is the one creature with whom I cannot Ssspeak. She either cannot hear, or refuses to answer, my questions. But I can hear her crying. Her despair... our despair... hasss sunken us all to the bottom of this dark Lake."

A murmur that sounded more like a collective moan traveled through the guards.

The King's face folded in upon itself as he listened to something that no one else could hear. Then he opened his eyes and looked directly at Celia.

"Now you have brought this reminder of sssunlight here... and..." the King pointed a single, shaking claw at the prism, "I can *hear* it," he whispered.

"Hear it?" Celia asked, bewildered.

"It sssssssssssssspeaks to me," he said, still staring transfixed by the prism.

"The prism speaks to you?" Celia repeated.

He nodded, trembling as his ears perceived the messages that only he could hear.

"What does it say?" Celia asked in barely a whisper. She

remained still, not daring to move a muscle.

"It tellsssssssss me that you can bring me my Queen," he replied with astonishment. The guards shuddered at this statement.

"I... I... don't know what you are talking about," Celia said. "We both know that your Queen died a long time ago."

"It says you can bring me my gentle, strong, fair Queen."

"No, I swear," Celia said shaking her head. "I don't know anything about where your Queen…" Celia's voice trailed off. The King looked at her without a trace of pity in his tortured, red eyes.

"Think, Sssssssssssssspeaker, think…" the King said.

"I don't know," she said.

"THEN FIGURE IT OUT!" he yelled, and suddenly his mind was made up. He looked around the room to his guards and gave his orders. "Seize the fox! Take it to the deepest chamber. Leave the despicable addict with the girl!"

"Wait!" Celia screamed as a team of guards stepped forward and roughly grabbed Tippit. Without much trouble they clamped down on her limbs with their strong claws and began dragging her away. Two guards held Celia and Otto back to keep them from rushing to Tippit's aid. Tippit's paws scrambled and scratched on the tile floor, her eyes strained wildly in her head, but she was no match for the guards. They quickly tied her muzzle with rope and wrapped a cloth bag over her head, rendering her helpless.

A damp, leathery hand clamped down across Celia's mouth to muffle her screams as she watched Tippit's frantic efforts to keep from being dragged away. When they finally forced Tippit through a door far at the other end of the hall, and the doors swung shut, the guards released Celia and Otto.

"TIPPIT!" Celia screamed. She turned to the Snapping Turtle

King. "Bring her back now!" she demanded.

"Do you wisssssshhhhhh to join her?" the King hissed. "We could ignore the prism, and end this all now, in accordance to my original plan."

"No," Celia said quietly, restraining herself.

"Then go," the King said. "Do what the prism tells me you can do. You have until sunrise to bring me my Queen, and then, and only then, will I release the fox," the King said. "If you fail, however, we turtles will take swift and immediate measures to learn just exactly how long that fox is able to hold her breath underwater. Do you understand?"

Celia could not respond. Otto was suddenly at her side. He pulled on her arm with surprising strength.

"Celia," he whispered. "Sunrise is a matter of hours. We have no time to waste."

Celia knew he was right. Without another word, she turned away from the Snapping Turtle King and began running back through the Great Hall. The Snapping Turtle King and all his guards watched as she and Otto dove back into the icy water. Then the King slumped back onto his throne and closed his eyes.

Keen was just picking clean the last of the mouse bones, when Celia burst through the water's surface and dragged her shaking body out of the Lake. Keen was momentarily shocked to stillness, one of his most often used defense mechanisms. When Otto's head also splashed into view, Keen shook off his fear and came to his senses.

"Where's the fox?" he screeched. Without answering, Celia grabbed her Keds away from Keen and began fumbling to get them on her feet.

"Celia, where are you going?" Otto panted after her, dragging his body out of the Lake.

"No time to explain," she yelled. "Stay here! I'll be back." She didn't wait for his reply as she stumbled up the dirt and gravel path toward the camp. She had an idea—or a hope, but she wouldn't be able to do it on her own. There was one thing for certain; she would need another set of hands—human hands.

29. Celia, Not Alice

Celia's clothes were dripping as she quietly opened the screen door to Violet's dorm. She gently shook Violet, who was immediately wide awake. She stifled a small yelp, but quickly relaxed when she recognized Celia. Celia motioned impatiently for Violet to follow her out of the dorm. Violet slipped out of her sleeping bag, and into some sandals. She wrapped a plaid bathrobe around her green pajamas and they crept behind the dorm and crouched in the bushes.

Before Celia could ask if Violet had gotten her note, Violet wrapped her arms around Celia in a massive hug that almost knocked the wind out of her.

"I am so sorry about your brother, Ce," she said into Celia's shoulder.

"Thanks," was all Celia could think to say.

The two girls hugged each other tightly in silence. Celia felt a little warmth start to replace some of the chill in her bones. Then Violet pulled away and looked at Celia with a skeptical eye.

"You're dripping wet," she said.

"Yeah…"

"Are you ok?" Violet asked.

"Actually, no. I really need your help with something," Celia said.

"Anything you need," Violet answered without hesitation.

"You might think I am a little crazy..." Celia said.

"Try me," Violet answered with that defiant flash in her eyes.

"I need you to help me break into the Chow Lodge attic..."

"I'm your girl," Violet said.

"Wait, I'm not finished yet...I'm looking for something that I need to bring to the Lake..."

"Okay," Violet said, looking a little less certain. "That's in the Rules Song, but okay. What are you looking for?"

"I'm not exactly sure, but I'll know it when I see it."

"And what are you doing with this you'll-know-it-when-you-see-it thing when we get it to the Lake?" Violet asked. Celia took a deep breath. She said the next part quickly, without stopping.

"I'm bringing it to the Snapping Turtle King who lives in a palace at the bottom of the Lake."

Violet just stared at her. Her facial expression remained unchanged.

"Saaaaaay that last part again," she requested, making a little rewinding motion with her fingers.

Celia repeated herself.

"*The Snapping Turtle King?*" Violet asked. "Who lives in a palace at the bottom of the Lake?" Her voice was barely audible.

Celia nodded. "I've been...well, I can..." She wasn't sure how to explain this.

"You can *what?*" Violet asked.

"I can talk to animals," Celia said finally. "I'm a Speaker...it's just for a short while... but for now, I can...and I've been sneaking out of camp almost every night to go to the woods with the animals. That's why I'm so tired all day!"

Silence.

Violet's eyes were as round as two of Jupiter's sixty-two confirmed moons.

"Does this…" Violet asked very slowly, "have anything to do with your brother?"

"Sort of," Celia said.

"Celia… this is…" Violet began shaking her head. Celia winced, waiting for Violet to tell her she was delusional, and begin yelling for someone, anyone, to come restrain her.

"…the *most amazing* thing I have *ever* heard…" Violet said. "Of course I will help you." Celia threw her arms around Violet and hugged her with relief.

"There's just one thing…," Violet said. "I can only do this if we've been fully introduced."

Celia smiled and nodded. "You are a tenacious girl, if nothing else," she said as she pulled back her sleeve and showed Violet the prism tied there.

"Well…?" Violet asked, placing her hands on her hips, and cocking her head to one side.

"Ok, ok. It finally worked," Celia said. Violet's eyes narrowed.

"Oh, cut the bull, Celia," she said. "We both know you've remembered this whole time. You were just holding out on me."

Celia smiled and shook her head. She liked this girl. She really, really did. Celia took a deep breath, and then said it.

"My mother named me Celia, not Alice, because she wanted me to be similar to Alice, but different. She wanted me to have Alice's curiosity, sweetness, and creativity, but she knew that I would need more than just that to get by in the real world. If you read Lewis Carroll's story very carefully, and we did many, many times, Alice is a slightly lazy daydreamer who becomes confused and helpless when she gets lost."

"My mother didn't want that for me. Besides having curiosity, sweetness, and creativity, she also wanted me to have confidence, intelligence, and strength."

Celia paused and thought about Otto.

"I guess a sort of 'fighter's quality' if you will," she added. Then she continued. "I didn't understand it at the time, but my mom always warned me that one day, just like Alice, I would get lost. She said that everyone loses their way at one point or another, even if you simply stay in the very same place you've always been. And I did. When Kyel died, I got very, very lost. And I still am, but now I understand that getting lost is also an adventure. It's Wonderland – scary, strange, disorienting, but also magical and beautiful. And thankfully my parents raised me to also have the confidence, intelligence, and strength to figure things out, because I'm not exactly an Alice – I'm slightly rearranged into Celia."

"Wow," Violet said quietly, and nodded. She grabbed Celia's hand and squeezed it.

"Alright, Celia-not-Alice," she said, an appreciative smile spreading across her face, "now that we've been properly introduced; let's do this."

Violet suddenly dropped into a sprinter's pose. Celia dropped down beside her.

"BANG!" Violet whispered.

Both girls began sprinting full speed down the Hedgehog Path toward the Chow Lodge.

30. The Chow Lodge Attic

Celia and Violet grabbed two flashlights and a ladder from the Slop Shop behind the Chow Lodge. Loud rumbling snores erupted from Rupert and George's pigpen. Celia heard one of them mumble something about the pointlessness of applesauce, but she continued working quickly and quietly, not wanting to wake them. Celia wasn't sure where Aggie and Ma slept, but she was sure that, if disturbed, Rupert and George's squeals could probably reach them.

Celia and Violet lugged the heavy wooden ladder in through the back door of the Chow Lodge. They stood for a moment in the large room, listening. It was empty and still. Celia tried to imagine the space around her as it had been decades ago, when it was the family home to Edith Glynwood and her father, Susan's great-grandfather. She looked up at the door in the rafters that had no stairs leading to it. She imagined a young girl, who no longer existed, running down the stairs, which no longer existed, to hug her father who also no longer existed.

Celia propped the ladder against the wooden wall. It just reached the landing that hovered in front of the attic door.

"Afraid of heights?" Celia asked. Violet shook her head.

"Good thing," she said.

In no time, both girls had shimmied up the ladder and were

standing on the narrow landing, looking back down at the Chow Lodge. Celia turned the door's handle. With a slight protest from the cranky hinges, it squeaked open.

"I guess there's no need to lock a door that's missing a staircase," Violet whispered.

With a *click* and a *click*, Celia and Violet illuminated their flashlights and stepped into the small, dark room. Some little creature did its best to scamper away from their approaching footsteps and light beams. Both girls froze instinctively.

Chipmunk, Celia thought. When the scratching noise settled and the room was still again, they entered.

If it were possible for a place to feel like a cavern and a cathedral at the same time, this room was it. It was small and cramped, but with a steeply tilting ceiling that made it feel larger than it really was. As their flashlights searched the room, the first things Celia noticed were the framed photographs hanging on the walls. There were photos, both in black and white and full color, of each building being constructed; Command Central, the Cupcake, the Dorms, the Dance Pavilion, all with brighter, yellower wood, surrounded by younger, shorter trees.

There were also dusty framed photographs of a tall woman with brown hair. The woman was surrounded by hundreds of smiling girls and women. Celia felt like she knew the woman in the pictures.

"Hello, Edith," she whispered.

Through the years, the woman grew older and older until her hair turned pure white, but her powerful smile always remained the same. She was always surrounded by other smiling girls who, over time, also grew into smiling women. A young Mrs. Nalgy grew into an older Mrs. Nalgy. Violet pointed to one picture that must have been Susan when she was about their age. Susan was smiling with a mouth full of braces, looking up at Edith who had her hand on Susan's shoulder and looked directly at the camera.

Celia pulled herself away from the pictures and scanned the attic's random collection of well-worn but loved objects. An old camping trunk sat next to a large, flaking mirror, a dusty conch shell, and a figurine of a dog with a clock on its chest. There was a small red snowsuit draped over a large, framed drawing of London's skyline at nighttime. Hanging on the walls beside the drawing was a small hatchet, and a pair of mounted and labeled goat horns.

Both girls began digging through the objects. Violet opened the doors of an old wardrobe and found nothing but four old fur coats and some dried pine needles. Celia found a shovel, a pick ax, some jars of preserved peaches. She moved aside an old pair of running shoes, round eyeglasses, and an old broom, to find something that looked like a toy astronaut helmet. Violet rummaged through a large stack of archery targets strewn next to a jumbled pile of dusty bows and quivers, to find a jar that contained many spools of thread, and another one that contained only black buttons.

"This it?" Violet asked shaking the jar of black buttons.

"No," Celia said distractedly, still searching. Finally, behind some empty boxes that were labeled chocolate bars, but now held a jumble of mixed-up files, Celia found a small bookshelf.

Filled with brown notebooks.

"Here!" she whispered to Violet, moving the boxes aside. "Help me find the notebook that has '1935' written inside the front cover." They began pulling notebooks from the shelf. They were in chronological order, so it didn't take long for Violet to give a little yelp and hand the right notebook to Celia.

Celia flipped open the front cover. It said, *"Edith Glynwood - 1935-1936."*

"This is the one!" Celia said. And she began flipping through the entries, stopping when she found what she was looking for. Celia trained her flashlight on the words and began reading out loud to Violet.

August 5, 1935

"How can a day be both so beautiful and so sad? I was waiting at the Lake's edge for my friend to meet me, when I heard desperate breathing. A few steps away, there was a large turtle in the sand. At first I thought she was resting in the sunshine, or laying eggs in the sand. But then I noticed her breathing was more like a gasping, and that each breath was more hollow than the one before.

I tried to speak with her, but she was too weak to reply, so I sat with her and did my best to comfort her. There was a little foam at her lips, which I wiped away. She looked at me with understanding and peace in her eyes. She was so strong and yet so fragile. Then, as I held her, she breathed one last breath, and died. At the moment when the life left her body, I felt peace. I was no longer afraid or angry for my father's death. I felt tears of relief streaming from my own eyes.

Just then, my friend arrived. We made attempts to speak, but couldn't. I was suddenly scared of her, and I think she feared me as well. I was still clutching the lifeless turtle when she turned and disappeared into the woods. I could not leave the turtle in the sand, alone to be dragged away and eaten by scavengers. I know that's the natural thing, but I couldn't stand to think of it. So I have taken her. I don't know if I will be able to explain what transpired to my friend. I don't know if I will see her again."

The entry ended there.

"She didn't kill the turtle," Celia said to herself. "The Queen died a natural death." Celia flipped through the other pages, and back again to this entry. "The Queen died naturally," she repeated. Violet sat quietly next to her.

"Is this what you need to bring to the King?" she asked.

"No," Celia said, thinking it over. "I don't think he would accept this journal. He wants the Queen." Celia peered around the attic's interior. "There must be something else here," she whispered.

Just then Violet's flashlight shined on Celia's wrist. The prism lit up like a glowing orb. Small rainbows scattered across the room and collected on the large camping trunk. The girls looked at each other with amazement. Celia jumped up and ran to the trunk. She attempted to heave it open, but it was locked.

Celia's eyes scoured the objects in the room and rested on the hatchet hanging on the wall. She grabbed it and in one swift motion, brought its rusted, dull blade down on the lock.

It fell open with a satisfying *click*.

Celia and Violet pulled open the heavy top and shined their flashlights inside. There, nestled safely between soft, cotton cloth, was a hollow turtle shell large enough to fit a Queen.

"Good evening, your majesty," Celia whispered, running a gentle finger down the spikey bumps on the shell. She studied the intricate pattern of the shell for a moment; it reminded her of moonlight dappling on water.

No; sunlight *dappling on water*, she thought, and smiled. Then she snapped back into action. Violet helped her cautiously lift the shell out of the trunk. They wrapped it inside an old sleeping bag for safe carrying. As they walked carefully toward the door, Violet stepped on a small rusted toy car and slipped. She dropped her flashlight, but managed to hang on to the shell. Celia helped Violet to her feet and handed her the flashlight.

"Here's to hoping we can get this down the ladder in one piece," Celia said, drawing a circle around her face with one finger, pulling her ears, and wiggling her elbows. Violet did the same.

Then Celia took one last look at the attic's eclectic contents, whispered thanks to Edith Glynwood, and closed the door behind them.

31. Susan's Pilot Light

Susan walked, still half asleep, into the Chow Lodge clutching an empty coffee mug, her clipboard, a wrench, and the correct replacement part for the stove. She took a quick drink of water straight from the tap, and then got down on her hands and knees preparing to wrestle with the dreaded stove.

She was wedged deep underneath the giant stove, fiddling with wires, and cursing quietly to herself, when she heard a loud *thump* from the floorboards above.

She froze and listened.

Chipmunks, she thought as she turned her attention back to the tiny screw she had just dropped. Then she heard more scuffling from above.

Susan pulled her head out from under the stove, and stood up just in time to see Celia and Violet exit the attic door and carefully shut it behind them.

She watched with shock as they began climbing down a large ladder propped against the wall. Susan was so surprised that she didn't even call out to them. She quietly put the wrench down next to her clipboard, and watched with open-mouthed fascination as they worked in tandem to descend the ladder with something quite large wrapped in a faded blue sleeping bag.

Susan hadn't seen Celia on her feet in four days. In fact, she was planning to call Mr. and Mrs. Johnson later that morning to suggest it might be for the best if they took Celia home when they came for Visiting Day next weekend. At least for a day or two. It was written on her list of things to do. But Celia certainly looked fine now. She was moving with purpose and strength. Susan watched as the two girls accomplished their goal together, whispering and working as a team. Despite herself, Susan felt a small flame of hope flicker to life in her chest. Then she closed her gaping mouth and quietly walked to block the front doors.

The girls safely reached the Chow Lodge's floor. They left the ladder standing right where it was, turned, and practically ran smack-dab into Susan as they tried to leave.

"Good almost morning, girls," Susan said quietly with a calm, neutral expression on her face. "And what have you got there?" she asked.

Celia and Violet stood perfectly still. Shocked, scared, and so incredibly disappointed.

No, Celia thought. *No, no, no, no, no! This is not happening. It cannot end here. It cannot.*

"Susan…" Celia said, but she didn't know what to say after that. She fell silent.

"Celia," Susan said. "I am very glad to see that you are feeling better." She turned and nodded to Violet. "And Violet, it's always lovely to see you."

Violet simply nodded in return, her mouth still hanging open. The three of them stared silently at each other for a moment.

"Well, what's in the sleeping bag?" Susan asked again. Violet couldn't say anything as tears began to well up in her eyes. Celia's mind raced, and then calmed. She was done hiding the truth from Susan.

"It's a snapping turtle shell," she said. Susan looked a little surprised, if not intrigued.

"And where are you planning to take that turtle shell?" she asked.

"To the Lake," Celia finally answered.

"The *Lake*?" Susan gasped, throwing her tough-love act aside for genuine surprise.

"Yes."

"Sneaking around camp at night is definitely breaking the rules," Susan said, "but going to the Lake, without an adult, is dangerous. And in the dark?!" She was genuinely upset.

Suddenly Violet let out a huge sob. "Please, don't send us home," she begged.

"Susan," Celia said. "Please don't let Violet get in trouble. It was my idea, and she was just trying to be a good friend and help me. I'll take all of the blame. I didn't mean any disrespect to you or the Rules Song, it's just that... there is something that I need to do, and if I told you, you would probably think I'm crazy...but it could help me, with...with things."

Susan looked at Celia. She was so relieved to see the girl on her feet and talking, that despite her first reaction, the tiny pilot light of hope continued to flicker inside her chest.

"What kind of *things*?" Susan asked, her voice softening.

"My brother..." Celia said. Susan nodded quietly.

Susan turned up the hope in her heart and allowed the little flame to grow brighter.

"What else?" she asked.

"It also involves your grandmother, Edith, I mean, Mrs.

Glynwood," Celia added. Susan raised both eyebrows.

"I'm not saying that as an excuse," Celia continued, "I just wanted you to know it was important...not just something for the sake of breaking rules."

Susan looked with bewilderment at the ladder and the turtle shell wrapped in the sleeping bag. She looked at Celia and Violet's honest and beautiful faces, and felt warmth filling her up, like a gentle, guiding hand on her heart. If her twenty-nine summers growing up at Camp Glynwood had taught her anything she thought, it was these two things: one - life would never cease to amaze her, and two - never, *ever* underestimate a child.

"Celia," she said softly. "I am so glad that you are back on your feet, and making friends...but I cannot allow you to go to the Lake."

Outside the sky was drifting into a brighter shade of lavender. Celia hung her head. She felt giant tears gathering in the sides of her squinted eyes.

So that was that, Celia thought. *It was over.* She would never get the shell to the Snapping Turtle King in time. She thought about Tippit, living the last hour of her life trapped somewhere in a damp, dark cell scared and waiting for Celia who would never return.

"At least," Susan said finishing her sentence, "not *alone.*"

Both Celia and Violet looked up at Susan with shock.

"I will come with you to the Lake," she said. Both of the girls gasped.

"The rules don't forbid swimming at *night*..." Susan clarified, "they forbid swimming *alone*, without an adult. As I recall, you both classified as Orcas, the highest level of independent swimmers. As long as I come with you to the Lake, it's ok."

Celia threw her arms around Susan and squeezed her with all

her might.

"Thank you," she said, wiping away her tears.

"And then maybe after your pre-dawn swim, you can explain what this is all about…" Susan added.

"Yes! Afterwards!" Celia yelled, as she and Violet pushed the Chow Lodge doors open, running with the sleeping bag between them. Without a further moment of hesitation, Susan ran after them leaving her clipboard behind on the floor.

32. Back to the Palace

It was a strange collection of animals and humans gathered at the waterfront. There was a shifty-eyed otter, a tiny owl almost comatose with fear, a jittery younger blond human, and a dazed older brunette.

Then there was Celia.

Her dark skin was shining in the moonlight, and her eyes filled momentarily with wonder as she looked over the unlikely gathering.

They are all here to help me, she thought. *I am not alone, and I never was.*

Each creature stared at the others in momentary disbelief. Then the small gathering erupted into confusion. Violet and Susan couldn't understand Otto or Keen, and they in return, couldn't understand Violet or Susan. Celia watched for a moment as chaos descended onto the small group.

Then she took charge.

"Susan!" she yelled over the din, "You'll stay here with Keen. Violet, you're coming with me and Otto." Again, they all spoke at once.

"But that's a real otter! Otters are fierce and unpredictable."

"Adult humans are killers! Never to be trusted!"

"These are mammals. Mammals carry rabies…"

"For the last time, where *is* the fox?!"

Celia rolled her eyes to the sky in exasperation, but when she did, she saw the first pink rays of sunlight reaching across the lavender sky. The sun was beginning to rise.

"Quiet!" Celia cried out, "We don't have time for this! Everyone remain calm. I trust each and every one of you, and I *need* each of you to trust each other."

Otto inspected Susan and Violet with shifty eyes and a string of curses that Celia was thankful they couldn't understand. Keen twittered in agreement and puffed his feathers to about three times his normal girth. Susan carefully sat down on the Lake's edge, tucking her feet and hands into her body to keep them safe from small jaws or talons that she thought might attack at any moment.

Violet was the only one who seemed to be enjoying herself.

"You can really talk to them, Ce?" she asked. Celia nodded.

She didn't want to mention it, but since they had come back down to the Lake, it was actually a little more difficult for her to understand them. Otto's grumbling and Keen's bickering were partially garbled with indistinguishable noises, but she pushed this observation aside in her mind for the moment.

"Come on, Ultra-V!" Celia said, motioning for Violet to follow her into the water.

"Right behind you, Celia-not-Alice," Violet whispered.

Otto, however, was frozen in place, still staring distrustfully at Susan and Violet.

"Let's go, Otto!" Celia yelled as she dragged the sleeping bag into the Lake and let it fill with water so that it would submerge more easily. A ray of sunlight pierced through the clouds. Otto spotted the signs of the fast-approaching dawn and snapped to. There was no time to fill empty bottles with air. They would just have to dive, and swim as quickly as possible.

"I'm with you, Celia," Otto said with determination, his stormy mood from a few seconds before now vanished.

"I'm not sure how I feel about this!" Susan yelled.

But before she could do anything about it, Celia dove down into the chilly water, cradling the gigantic sleeping bag. Otto and then Violet followed behind her, leaving Susan and Keen on the shore, stunned into blinking silence.

Underwater, Violet caught up to Celia and helped her drag the sleeping bag along. Otto helped by pushing from behind. The water still had the same dreadful chill, but somehow Celia felt much stronger this time. Maybe it was having Violet with her, maybe it was being in charge, but with each powerful stroke of her arms and kick of her legs, Celia covered more and more distance.

However, dawn was fast approaching. Unlike before, as they moved closer and closer towards the bottom of the Lake, the water around them grew lighter and lighter. By the time they reached the forest of underwater trees, Celia could see that the sunrise had begun.

They rocketed towards the entrance of the Snapping Turtle King's palace, towing the sleeping bag behind them. Celia led them through the large underwater doors and charged out of the water. She helped Otto and Violet onto the slick algae rocks, and together they dragged the dripping sleeping bag towards the great hallway. Violet stood with her mouth hanging open for a moment, looking around the massive, hollow tree lit with flickering lanterns.

"What is this place?" she gasped.

"No time!" Celia whispered, as she grabbed Violet's hand. They ran down the long hallway, carrying the sleeping bag, which now felt as if it was at least three times its original weight.

Just before they reached the large doors to the Great Hall, Celia gave Violet the sleeping bag and motioned for her to hide inside a nook right behind one of the great doors.

"Stay here and wait for my signal," she said. Violet nodded, clutching the sleeping bag to her chest. Celia grabbed Otto's paw, and without ringing the bell, pushed open the doors to the Great Hall.

"Hello?!" Celia yelled. The guards stood as they did before, but the throne was empty.

"Yooooou whooooo, Cyrus!" Otto yelled.

Before Celia had time to call again, a familiar hissing noise emerged from the shadows beside them.

"Ssssssssssssssssssssoooooooooooooooo..." it said, "The Sssssssssssssssssssspeaker returns!"

Otto and Celia turned to see the Snapping Turtle King. He was inspecting the piles of turtle bones that covered the walls of the Great Hall. He ran a clawed finger along one of the sharp beaks on a hollow skull. It made a long, empty, scratching sound. He looked down the empty Hallway to the pool of water at the Palace entrance. It was a bright shade of green, shimmering with sunlight.

"You have failed, Sssspeaker," the Snapping Turtle King said, quietly, almost completely void of emotion, except for the smallest tinge of disappointment. "The sun hasss already begun to risssse."

"But I have what you asked for," Celia said.

"I sssssee nothing," the King replied, carefully inspecting Celia and Otto.

"Let Tippit go," Celia said calmly, "and then I will give you the Queen."

The King shook his head, almost with pity. "You have nothing, Ccccelia," he said, using her name for the first time. "You would have been much wiser to stay away, because for nothing, you shall pay with your friends' lives, *and* your own." The King raised a clawed finger, preparing to give the next command to his guards.

"Violet!" Celia yelled.

Trembling, Violet stepped out from behind the large door, grasping the dripping wet sleeping bag. She dropped into a sprinter's pose, and before any of the guards could move, she dashed to Celia and Otto's side, and placed the bag between them. They shifted to form a protective triangle around it.

"What isss that?" the King hissed. He took a quick step forward, his claws click-clacking, and the guards took a collective step closer toward the center of the room.

"What is he saying?" Violet whispered.

"Just stay calm," Celia muttered quietly, "and follow my lead..."

"For the love of mutated guppies and eel slime..." Otto grumbled, gnashing his small, sharp teeth at the snapping turtles. "Don't take another step closer..." he warned.

"WHAT IS THAT?!" the King bellowed. He was trembling all over, reaching a single, shaking claw towards the sleeping bag.

"First, let Tippit go," Celia replied in a firm voice.

"Or what?" the King asked.

"Or I will smash the contents of the sleeping bag," Celia said. She daringly raised a single foot high above the sleeping bag and threatening to bring it down with a powerful blow.

"Releasssssssse the fox!" the Snapping Turtle King yelled. A pair of doors in the back of the Great Hall thundered open and guards entered, pulling a bag off of Tippit's head. Tippit was shaking, and blinking in the light, but she regained her bearings quickly, and scrambled to Celia's side. Celia reached down and quickly ruffled the fur on Tippit's neck. She was damp and trembling, but uninjured.

"And s-s-s-ssssssssoo…?" the King could barely stammer, trembling now from the top of his spiky head to the tip of his long, thin tail.

Celia nodded with satisfaction. With Violet and Otto's help, she reached into the sleeping bag and pulled out the giant turtle shell. They placed it gently onto the ground, and stepped away.

The King uttered a weak gasp. A loud clattering noise erupted through the hall as every guard dropped to his knees and bowed his head. Then, the Great Hall was perfectly silent.

The Snapping Turtle King walked slowly to the shell.

"Talia," he whispered, "My Queen…"

He reached out a quivering claw to gently touch the shell, and as he did, a blank expression washed over his face. Celia could see from the look in his eyes that for him there was no longer anything else in the room, or perhaps even the universe. He had been transported a million miles away, and a hundred years in the past, or perhaps the future, and nothing could bring him back to this present moment or place.

Suddenly, the prism on Celia's wrist began to radiate with light. An airy and tinkling sound filled the Palace. A sparkling mist, filled with flashes of sunlight refracted into colorful beams, slowly descended on the shell. The King stood back and blinked, unbelieving, as the shell slowly transformed into the majestic Snapping Turtle Queen. She stood tall and proud with beautifully wrinkled skin, and eyes flickering with joy. She turned, a tattered white dress flowing gently around her, and faced the Snapping Turtle King with open arms.

"Cyrus," she whispered, and the King stepped forward to hold her gently, rested his head on her shoulder and closed his eyes.

"What is going on?" Celia whispered, staring at the Snapping Turtle King and Queen embracing. "How is that happening?" she asked.

Violet smiled. "He is remembering," she said.

Celia watched as the Queen took one of her clawed fingers and brushed away a tear from the King's face. She whispered something in his ear that no one else could hear. Then she kissed his rough leathery cheek, and something shadowy and foul lifted out of him and drifted away.

The King opened his eyes, and Celia saw that they held something new. It was the expression of a creature who had treasured and loved someone so preciously dear, that to lose her was so painful he would need to bury everything good about himself in order to survive a life lived without her. But with one touch, one true remembering, the memories of love and happiness came back, along with his true self, his good self.

The King and Queen began to dance, softly swaying back and forth, in a simple waltz. The guards, still kneeling, watched in awe, some of them weeping.

Violet turned to Celia with a large smile spread across her face. But Violet saw that Celia was still confused. Suddenly, Violet's eyes flashed. She grabbed both of Celia's hands and ran with her to the center of the Great Hall. She began twirling them both around in circles, joining the King and Queen in their waltz.

"What are you doing, V?" Celia asked.

"Close your eyes," Violet said.

"No, really. What are you doing?" Celia insisted.

"Remembering is easier if you have an object, but it's not entirely necessary," Violet said. "Close your eyes!"

Celia closed her eyes.

"Now... think about Kyel, really think about him. Picture his face, and his eyes, and his shoulders, and the way he stood. What was his shoe size? And his favorite t-shirt? What was his least favorite song? And the toy he kept with him at night? What did his voice sound like after he cried? What was his biggest fear? What did he want to be when he grew up?"

"I don't know..." Celia said, overwhelmed by the spinning and the questions.

"Yes, you do, Celia," Violet whispered. "You just have to let go and remember."

"What did he smell like, Celia?" Otto's voice chimed in. "Think about his smell until you can smell it again," he urged. Celia let her mind go, and began searching in the dark corners for what she had held herself back from remembering.

"What did his eyes look like when he smiled?" Tippit's voice asked her. Their voices sounded like they were getting farther away. Celia began to picture Kyel.

"What did his laugh sound like?" Violet called. "What did it feel like when you laughed together?" Her voice now sounded like it was miles and miles away on the other side of a cloudy horizon.

"His laugh..." Celia said quietly to herself, "his laugh sounded like summers in Jamaica...running through the big leaves, and splashing through the streams. His skin smelled like coconuts...no, like two eggs frying sunny-side up in coconut oil, and his smile...his smile looked like a crescent moon rising above the ocean, and it felt as warm and mysterious as your feet buried in the toasty sand after the sunset...When we laughed together it felt like real freedom, like flying, effortlessly..."

"Open your eyes," Violet whispered.

Celia opened her eyes. Standing before her, was Kyel.

33. The Remembering

"KYEL!" Celia cried out.

And there he was; his tiny, wiry body almost as tall as hers; his skin the same color of dark hot chocolate before you add the marshmallows; his hair a wild, giant puff, like the top of an ebony dandelion ready to fly away in the wind.

He smiled up at her with twinkling eyes, and shrugged his shoulders in his simple way.

Celia pulled his tiny body into a strong hug, and breathed deeply. He hugged her back with all his strength, and she felt the warmth of the sun return to her heart.

"I love you, Ky," she whispered.

"I love you, Ce," he replied in his own beautiful, happy voice, clear and real as truth.

Celia pulled away and looked at her brother. She knew it wasn't really him, not like she knew him before, but it was him as she would know him from now on. Not a ghost, not a dream, but the real Kyel, somehow just beyond the visible spectrum, but somehow just as real. Kyel laughed, and without knowing why, Celia began to laugh too. She felt so much better already.

"Shall we dance?" he asked, grinning his sly grin.

Celia rested her forehead on the top of Kyel's head and closed her eyes. Slowly they began waltzing, spinning and rocking back and forth. Celia thought of all the things she wanted to say to Kyel, but instead, she felt a quiet peace wash over her. She held his memory in her strong embrace and thought about the boy he was, and the man that he would never grow up to be. She thought about how every adventure she would ever have with Kyel, had already happened. And how there would never be any new ones. But then, instead of feeling sad, she felt thankful. Thankful that she had ever known him. Thankful that he was ever her brother.

"Ce, look," Kyel said.

Celia opened her eyes and saw that Violet was also dancing. But her friend's feet were not touching the floor. She was wrapped in the warm embrace of a very tall, thin man, holding her in a tight hug. The man's hair was light blond like hers, and as he looked at Violet, his bright blue eyes flashed defiantly with love. Violet's eyes were closed, and Celia watched as her friend held her ear to her father's chest, listening to his breath and his heartbeat, with a calm, peaceful smile.

Celia looked around the Great Hall and saw that Otto was standing silently alongside a larger otter who had placed a paw gently on his shoulder. And Tippit was accompanied by a slightly larger red fox, her sister, who was busily grooming Tippit between her ears.

Then as they all, the guards included, swayed together, the Great Hall began to tilt and shift under the weight. Bubbles formed and rose in the entrance pool, and a tremor ran through the walls. Slowly, the palace dislodged from the murky Lake bottom, and began to rise.

At first, the giant structure moved slowly, but soon it gathered speed, moving faster and faster. The stacks and stacks of snapping turtle bones began to chatter and rattle. Chunks of the ceiling began to fall in, allowing water to rush through the new holes. Celia and the others looked around, beginning to fear that the whole Palace would be destroyed and crush them all. But suddenly, with a noise that sounded as if the Palace itself gave a huge sigh of relief, it crashed through the Lake's surface, and bobbed peacefully in the open water.

All the inhabitants of the Great Hall looked around themselves with amazement as the water drained away from their feet, and they breathed in the fresh air. They gazed out into the great open sky where there was a celestial orb resting on each horizon, the moon setting in the West, and the sun rising in the East.

The Palace floated serenely toward the shore. A few feet away, Susan stood in disbelief. Keen perched on her shoulder to get a better view.

Slowly, the tinkling, glowing mist of remembering drifted to them too, and suddenly, Keen was soaring and dive-bombing through the air with his family, and Susan was holding hands with an older woman with white hair, Edith, her grandmother, who looked back at her with eyes brimming with pride.

The Snapping Turtle Queen nodded to Edith with a gentle smile. Edith nodded back, returning the gratitude. Then they both turned to Celia and smiled.

The birds were beginning to sing. As their sweet, hopeful song welcoming the dawn grew louder and louder, Celia felt something welling up inside of her that grew stronger and stronger, until she could no longer hold it in.

She grabbed Kyel's hand, and stepped into the Lake's shallow waters. Then she lifted her head to the rising sun and released the loudest, wildest, howl of her life. It was a sad sound, of primal sorrow for what had been lost, but also a beautiful sound, filled with joy and wonder for all the love that was there. Kyel raised his head to the sky and answered with his own powerful, eardrum-piercing howl. Then Violet and her father joined in with their own howls, and Cyrus and Talia. Soon everyone was howling; Tippit and her sister, Keen and his family, Otto and his father, Susan and Edith Glynwood, even the guards. Their howls rose high above them and drifted through the morning air.

Far across the hilltops, Anayla perked her large, furry ears to the wind. She stood quickly, and lifted her head to the rising sun. She returned the howls, and was joined by the rest of her pack, and the three kits, giving their thanks that Celia had succeeded.

Even farther away, the Lynx stood on the mountain crest outside his cave. He did not howl in response, but closed his eyes, and listened carefully to all the different voices raised in unison, and was glad to know that all was well again.

34. The Silence

When the last howl was flung at the rising sun, and silence finally settled upon the group, Celia opened her eyes to see that Kyel was gone. So was the Snapping Turtle Queen, Violet's father, and all the other memories. It was just the living gathered around, still stunned and looking at each other.

"Way to go, Celia-not-Alice," Violet whispered softly.

Celia shook her head, wishing she could still hug Kyel's little body.

"Will I be able to do it again?" she asked.

Violet nodded. "It will be different every time. But whenever you really need to speak to Kyel, just close your eyes and remember him. Remember every tiny little thing you know and love about him…and you can be with him again," she said.

"Thank you," Celia said, taking Violet's hand. She slipped the prism off her wrist and tied it back around Violet's neck. Violet smiled and nodded. Together, they walked out of the water to Susan who was standing just a few feet away on the shore.

A loud bubbly sound came from behind them, and they turned to watch as the snapping turtle guards towed the Palace across the Lake and moored it on a sandy beach hidden under a weeping willow tree, the place where the Queen had died.

But Cyrus was not with them. He had tossed his crown aside, and was slowly swimming across the Lake on his back, gazing up at the sunbeams streaking across the sky, half-humming-half-singing a soft melody. Celia listened carefully and realized that she couldn't understand any of the words.

Then Keen made a loud screeching noise in her ear, and Otto emitted a squeaky, whining noise from his throat.

Celia knew her Speaker powers were gone.

"Tippit!" she yelled and ran to throw her arms around the fox. Tippit looked deep into Celia's eyes, and smiled, but did not attempt to say a word.

Keen landed on Celia's shoulder and gave her ear a friendly nibble. She pet his head gently and he cooed quietly. Then he flapped his tiny wings and soared into the air.

Next, Otto stepped forward. There was a new peace in his eyes. He nudged the three bottles of Rubbing Alcohol toward Susan. She eyed them, incredulously, shaking her head with disbelief. With a twinkle in his eye, and a last shake of his whiskers, he dove back into the Lake and began swimming to the other side, toward the otter colony. Keen soared above him, swooping and diving to touch the water with his talons, sending ripples across the surface.

Soon it was just Celia, Violet, Susan and Tippit standing dripping wet by the water's edge, looking at each other.

"My brain doesn't fully understand what just happened," Susan finally said, breaking the silence, "but I think my heart does. Thank you so much for sharing this with me," she said, and pulled Celia and Violet into a warm hug. The girls hugged Susan back as hard as they could.

Then Violet pulled Susan away from Celia. They looked down at Tippit who was still resting by Celia's heels, her tail wrapped daintily around her paws. Violet gave Tippit's head a gentle pat, then tugged at Susan to walk with her back up the hill, leaving Celia alone with the fox.

Celia and Tippit sat side by side in silence at the edge of the Lake for a long time. Tippit rested her head in Celia's lap, and Celia ran her fingers through Tippit's long fur. They looked over the smooth surface of the water reflecting the endlessly deep blue sky above them. Neither tried to speak. They simply enjoyed being together.

Finally, when the Time Gong rang out over the hill behind them, Celia knew there would be other campers waking up. She turned to Tippit and plunged her face deep into her fur and hugged her tightly, breathing in the sweet smell of her earthy skin. Tippit nuzzled into the crook of Celia's arm and licked her.

Tears blurred Celia's vision when she let go of Tippit's neck. She stared deeply into her friend's golden-yellow eyes. Tippit looked back at Celia serenely, and without a sound, winked once. Celia winked back, then watched as her friend turned, and in a flash of orangey-red, disappeared into the woods.

35. Visiting Day

Celia was in the middle of a beautiful dream, swimming in the clear Jamaican waters with Kyel and Tippit. Otto and somehow Keen were also swimming alongside them, and then, just as it can happen in dreams, they all leapt out of the water and began flying. Celia could feel the wind rushing past her sides as they soared through the air, higher and higher above the turquoise, sparkling ocean and green coconut trees, effortlessly turning in somersaults, laughing all the while. Giant whales jumped gracefully in and out of the water far below them, splashing huge waves of water that sparkled like a thousand prisms in the sunlight. Celia and Kyel had just followed Keen into a fearless spiraled dive-bomb plummet, skimming along the water, and playfully splashing Tippit and Otto, when suddenly Celia was awoken by someone jumping onto her cot.

"Celia! Wake up, wake up!" Violet yelled, bouncing on Celia's bed. "Visitors will be here in two hours!" she yelled, practically ricocheting through the ceiling with excitement. Celia pushed Violet away, and she tumble-rolled to the floor and bounced onto her feet. Violet grabbed Celia's empty duffle bag.

"Where are your clothes?" she chirped.

"Check the drawers," Celia said.

"Finally," Violet said with a sigh of mock-exasperation. She grabbed a pair of cut-off jean shorts and a white V-neck t-shirt from the drawers and flung them at Celia. Celia slipped them on inside her sleeping bag.

"Hey, Violet!" Samantha yelled from the other side of the dorm. "How do you always have so much energy?" Samantha had one leg propped up on a ledge in the wall, and she was trying to force a brush through her long, tangled hair. She had announced at the beginning of last week that the best thing about going to regular summer camp, instead of ballet camp, was only having to brush your hair twice the whole time; once on Visiting Day, and once on the last day. Now she was regretting it a little bit.

Violet shrugged her shoulders and smiled at Samantha. Samantha laughed, shaking her head.

"I don't know, Celia," Samantha continued. "You and I should figure out how to harness Violet's energy somehow...we could solve the world's energy crisis or something."

"I know. Talk about a renewable resource," Celia added. She slipped out of bed and then put on her Dodgers sweatshirt.

"Are you seriously going to wear that thing every day?" Samantha asked, staring at it. Celia shrugged.

"Yeah. Probably still for awhile at least," she said. Samantha squinted her eyes and nodded.

"I can respect that," she said.

Celia had ended up in the same drama class with Samantha during the last Activities Rotation. She quickly figured out that Samantha wasn't the stuck up ballet dancer she had mistaken her for during the first few days of camp. In fact, Samantha had been shy and hurt because she thought Celia didn't want to be her friend. Celia and Samantha picked each other as partners for the Drama class's final performance. They decided to act out a scene from *Alice's Adventures in Wonderland*, the one between Alice and the Caterpillar.

Samantha had suggested that Celia be Alice because of her name, but Celia insisted on taking the role of the Caterpillar instead. Samantha choreographed and taught Celia a beautiful dance sequence for when the caterpillar transforms into a butterfly. In the end, the two girls liked the dance part so much that they rewrote the ending so that both the Caterpillar and Alice grow flowing butterfly wings and fly away. The whole camp gave them a standing ovation.

Celia climbed out of bed and reached her hand into her shorts pocket to feel something crinkly. She pulled out a wadded up piece of paper. She unfolded it carefully for inspection. It was the return bus schedule from the Catskill Mountains to Manhattan's Port Authority Bus Station.

"What's that?" Violet asked, eyeing Celia. Celia crumpled the paper again and threw it into the garbage bin by the door.

"Trash," she said.

"Come on, Ce," Samantha called. "We gotta get Violet out of here before she busts a hole through our roof." The three girls barreled out of the Dorm Lucky Number 13 and ran barefoot down the Hedgehog Path to the Chow Lodge.

A few hours later, Celia was sitting alone on a swing by the Great Swamp keeping an eye on the main entrance when she saw her parents pull up in a rental car. Her mother was wearing a beautiful, long fuchsia dress. Her dad was wearing one of his white, summer linen shirts. He placed his arm around his wife's waist and led her towards the Sign-In table that Susan had set up by Command Central.

"Mr. and Mrs. Johnson!" she heard Susan say, standing up and walking around the table to shake their hands. But before Susan could reach them, Celia had flown across the Great Swamp and wrapped herself into a large, warm hug between both of her parents. They laughed and pulled her in closer, shaking Susan's hand above her head.

Later, after Celia had shown her parents the Nesting Grove, and introduced them to Violet, Samantha, and every other Glynwood Girl they passed, she brought them down to the Lake, and sat with them next to the Ducky Hut. Celia's mom had taken a comb out of her purse and was re-touching a few of Celia's braids that had come loose. When Celia was little, she'd hated this, but overtime she had grown to love the gentle tug and pull of her mom working on her hair. Her dad was telling her about a new colleague who had joined the x-ray team at the hospital, and her mother told her she would be teaching sixth grade English in September, instead of fourth grade. They interrupted and embellished each other's stories as they caught her up on the news from the apartment building and around the block. And then, as Celia's mom finished touching up the last braid, a silence settled over their conversation.

Celia realized the silence would probably always return to her family from time to time. It was the moment that each of them thought about who was missing, and could no longer contribute to the conversation. It was their natural signal that they all missed Kyel. Celia decided she could live with this – but only if the silence was a short pause, and not a long, stifling silence like the one that had descended on their apartment earlier that spring.

"I'm sorry," Celia said.

"For what?" her parents both asked at the same time.

"For being mad at you both when Kyel drowned. And for pretending to think that he hadn't died," Celia said.

"It's okay, sweetheart," her mother said. "We were...still *are* all dealing with Ky's death the best we can. I don't think any of us really knew what to do right after it happened."

"We made mistakes too, sweetheart," her dad said.

"What do you mean?" Celia asked.

"We probably rushed a few things, because we were just so turned around by our sadness," he explained.

"Like what?" Celia asked.

"Well," her mom continued, "we brought a few of the boxes back up from the basement storage," she explained, "you know, so that we still have a few of Ky's things around the house."

Her father smiled. "We know he is gone, but, he doesn't have to be completely gone," he said. Celia just nodded, knowing exactly what they meant.

"We brought you something, Ce," her mother said. She reached into her pocket and pulled out a small dinosaur carved out of a green coconut shell. She handed it to Celia.

"Thank you," Celia said, holding it in her hand, rubbing her fingers against the little ridges on its back and along its teeth. She knew it was a dinosaur, because that was what Kyel had told her the day he carved it, but she couldn't help think that it also looked a little like a fox.

"I'm not sure what you'll actually *do* with it," her mom said, laughing softly, shaking her head though her tears.

"Oh, I do," Celia said. "I'm going to string it on some leather and wear it around my neck," she said.

Her father smiled. "Good idea, Ce," he said.

"I've been thinking about something else, too," Celia said. "I think we should make a special family trip to Jamaica this winter, and spread Kyel's ashes at Gran's place. I think he would like to be there."

Both her parents smiled.

"That will be really nice, Ce," her father said. "Really nice." He took out a wad of tissues from his pocket, and passed them around.

"Been carrying these things everywhere," he chuckled bravely through his tears. After a few minutes of holding each other, they blew their noses, and exhaled those big sighs you do when you're done crying.

Just then the Time Gong sounded off twelve times. Her parents looked at each other, slightly confused.

"Come on," Celia said pulling her parents to their feet. "We are meeting Violet and her mother by the Chow Lodge for lunch. And I need to introduce you to Aggie and Ma. Aggie has this amazing hot sauce that you need to try. It's going to knock your socks off and leave them singed in the corner. After that, we need to stop by the Cupcake so that you can meet Mrs. Nalgy…"

"The Cupcake?" her mom asked, looking intrigued.

"You'll see when we get there…and then I want to show you what I started making in Sculpture Shop…it's not finished yet, but Violet and I and few of the other girls are working on it together. It's massive! I'm not even actually sure it will fit inside once we put all the pieces together."

Mr. and Mrs. Johnson smiled at each other over Celia's head.

"What?" she asked, wanting in on the smile.

"Well," Celia's dad said, "we were a little worried on the drive up this morning. We weren't sure if sending you to camp had been the right thing to do," he explained.

Celia laughed sheepishly. "Truth be told, it was pretty rough in the beginning. I did try to run away on the first night," she confessed.

"You *what?!*" her mom exclaimed.

"How'd that work out?" her dad asked, chuckling again, shaking his head.

"Well, I guess you could say it was pretty adventurous," Celia said. She smiled, and gave her mom a shy, sideways glace. "A kind of *Wonderland*, of sorts," she added. She studied her mom's face to see if she would understand.

Mrs. Johnson suddenly stopped walking. She dropped to her knees and grabbed her daughter's face between her hands. New tears gathered as Mrs. Johnson looked deep into Celia's eyes.

"Yeah," Celia added. "You were right, Mom. I *did* get pretty lost. And I still am a little bit. But I know I'm going to find my way again. 'Cause you know, I'm Celia, not Alice."

Mrs. Johnson stared at her daughter, searching and scanning everything there, the way only a mother can.

"I am so proud of you, baby," she finally said. Celia nodded, and understood that she really was. Then Mrs. Johnson gave a little laugh of amazement, and allowed her husband to help her back to her feet.

Mr. Johnson handed her another tissue from his pocket.

"What did I tell you about these things?" he asked.

The three of them began walking uphill to the Chow Lodge. As they approached the steepest part of the incline, they linked arms and carried on. Suddenly, Celia felt her heart just brimming over with gratitude and love. And if she wasn't sure before, she was positive at that moment, that the sunlight warming their backs and drying their tears was actually Kyel's strong, loving arms, helping his family climb the hill.

Celia turned and gave him a wink.

About the Author

Micah was born in Devon, England and raised in New York City and the Hudson Valley. She teaches 5th grade Humanities at the public school Arts & Letters in Brooklyn, NY. Her poetry has been published in *Chaparral Poetry Magazine* and her short play, *The Whippoorwill*, was produced and performed at Electric Lodge in Venice, CA. Micah currently lives in Bed-Stuy, Brooklyn with her husband, filmmaker Tore Knos, and their two daughters.

For more information about what Micah
is reading and writing, visit:

www.micahhales.com

47554953R00143

Made in the USA
Lexington, KY
10 August 2019